Selena's Magica Somnia

Book 2: *The Sun and the Sea*

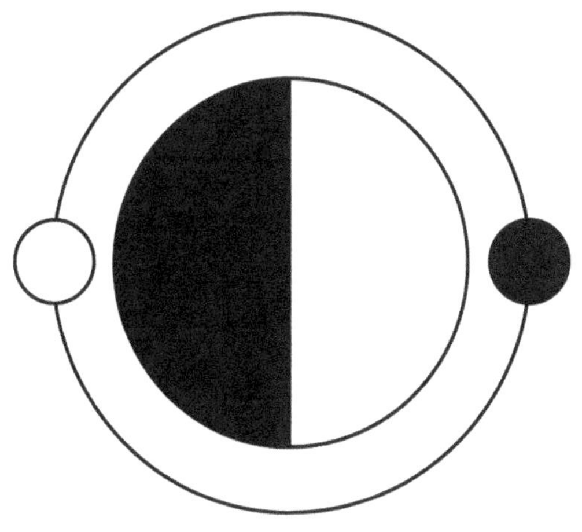

A.V. Dawn

Dedicated to the love of my life, Taylor

Those who create art are wonderful, special people, but those who inspire art are truly magical. You are the inspiration for all that I create, and I take great joy in creating worlds for us to explore together. I love you, and I will always be grateful for you sharing your magic with me.

I.

Lyra

I stumble through the dark woods, tripping over roots that have claimed the narrow path many years ago, following the sound of crashing waves. The full moon rests high in the sky, acting as my guide. The world is cold and bright in the moonlight but bleached of color, casting everything in shades of blue and gray as I race forward.

There it is again on my left hand—a black tattoo of a crescent moon surrounded with a ring and geometric line art. The Sigil of the Crescent Moon.

I skid to a halt, stopping at the edge of a cliff overlooking the ocean. In the distance, over the turbulent waters, two women levitate in the air, facing each other.

One wears a snow-white witch's hat and a long, white fur cloak that blows wildly in the winds. She brushes a strand of her straight, bluish-black hair from her piercing crystal-blue eyes that seem to glow unnaturally in the moonlight. She bears the Sigil of the Full Moon on her left hand—an orb representing the moon, surrounded with a snowflake pattern—so similar to the one on my own, yet entirely different all the same.

The other is tall and dark, leaner than her enemy. Her golden eyes are like stars in the night, her hair wild and curly around her round face. She wears a sleeveless black tailcoat with a gold lining, and her black witch's hat is adorned with gold trim. From her shoulder to her wrist, her right arm is covered in line-art tattoos of different beasts—a lion, an eagle, a rooster, a dragon—and upon her right hand is the Sigil of the Sun, a black symbol crafted in the sun's image.

"Yukiko!" I hear a man shout from the beach down below.

He is perhaps thirty, and taller than any man I've ever seen. He is fit, with long, wild brown hair and a short beard. His long black coat flaps around aggressively, the bottom half drenched from the waves. He, too, has the Sigil of the Full Moon on his left hand.

Both women raise their marked hands at each other, and the forces of nature respond to their call. A great globe of fire forms between them, utterly dwarfing them in scale, and flies at the white-clad witch. The ocean below stirs and the waves crash chaotically, until it spits up a pillar of water that reaches the very clouds above to intercept. The water swallows the flame, then descends back to the vicious sea.

In return, a great tsunami comes up to swallow the golden witch—a wall of water as tall as mountains. But the wave crashes back down to the sea harmlessly, clouds of steam wafting from the golden witch.

In the sky a dark mirage of the sun forms, its surface stirring with hot energy. A black solar flare shoots off toward the white-clad witch, who encases her form in a thick chunk of ice. The scalding blast shatters the frozen shell as it passes, leaving her unharmed.

Both women summon the energy of the celestial powers above them to their palms, and as they do, the moon and the dark sun both seem to glow more intensely.

Silver and gold bursts of power collide.

The world blares a blinding white, and I throw a hand up to cover my eyes—

And just like that, I'm back in my bedroom.

I let out a loud groan. It seems like I've had this same dream every night this week, and every time I do, it leaves a lingering feeling in my chest, like something is wrong.

I raise my left hand, expecting to see the sigil, but it's blank. I inspect my hand for a while, with only the light from the streetlamps outside to illuminate my room. It feels odd, almost as if I'm wearing another person's skin. I feel like a passenger in this body.

I sit up and look around the mint-colored room. I don't feel like I belong here. The desk beneath the window, the nightstand with the beige alarm clock, even the calendar on the back of the door, none of it feels like it's mine. I drag myself out of bed and walk over to the tall mirror hanging off the back of the walk-in closet door.

All the air flees my lungs and I recoil at the image I see looking back at me. For a split second, a dark-haired girl with blue eyes and a purple outfit looks back at me, but by the time I blink, she's gone, and only my startled form remains. I touch my face and my auburn hair, inspecting my reflection for any sign of disparity.

Perhaps I'm more tired than I realize. Still, I can't will myself back to sleep, so, instead, I get ready for school. I don't remember having to wear a uniform in the past, but the dark blue vest, matching plaid kilt, and white blouse do at least suit me.

As I change, I feel a sense of dread seeing the cracks on my left arm. They run from my elbow in all directions, as far as my wrist and my shoulder. They don't hurt, but they seem to be spreading, and they are sharp to the touch, as if running my fingertips along broken glass.

Maybe I should tell someone, or go to the doctor, but something inside me balks at the thought. I shake my head.

I walk over to the desk, where a silver ring with a crescent moon cradling a blue topaz lies. It's the only thing I have that actually feels like it belongs to me. I slip it on my left ring finger, something in my chest easing my anxieties.

I grab my navy winter coat, wrap a black wool scarf around my neck, and head downstairs to slip on my black cinch-top winter boots. My black canvas schoolbag sits by the door, and I sling it lazily over my shoulder and head out my door.

There is fresh snow covering the sidewalk, as pretty as it is slippery. The cold wind penetrates my leggings effortlessly, but the chill is still manageable.

I feel out of place in this neighborhood. All week, I keep getting my house number and street mixed up. I feel like I'm on the wrong side of town. I get all turned around walking to school, and it always feels weird how much longer my route seems to be.

I can see the back of the school as I turn a corner, looming at the end of the street. I'm early—the front gates won't even be open for another fifteen minutes or so. Even as I walk around the south wall of the grounds to the front, only a few cars rest in the parking lot, and the groundskeeper is still shoveling the snow away.

As I approach the iron-wrought front gates, I half-expect to see a cheerful ginger-haired girl with glasses and a tall boy with dark eyes, but no one is there. It's strange—I don't know anyone who fits those descriptions, yet somehow something in me always seems to be looking for them.

"You're here early, Lyra," a voice says to my left. I ignore it. "Lyra?"

I turn to see a middle-aged man in slacks and a nice tie shivering inside his rider jacket. He has a brown crew cut and round glasses.

The name seems so unfamiliar and ill-fitting, I often forget to respond when I hear it. It feels like someone else's.

Someone else's name. Someone else's home. Someone else's body. Is there anything in this life that's actually mine, other than this ring?

"Lyra, I'm talking to you," the man says, interrupting my thoughts.

"Sorry, sir, I wasn't paying attention," I reply.

"If you keep your head in the clouds you're bound to trip," he says with a smirk. He unlocks the gates and pulls them open with a heavy heave. "Get inside and warm up."

I drift through my classes aimlessly, almost like a ghost. I don't engage with the lessons, I don't talk to my classmates, and most people seem to ignore me, too. It feels like I'm a part of the background more than anything else, and by the time the final bell rings, I still can't shake this feeling of being out of place.

I linger after school, for no reason other than to avoid going back to that empty house. My parents are supposed to be away on a trip for December, but somehow, any time I try to think of them, I can only see blurry faces and unspecific shapes. I seem to have trouble recalling anything, for that matter. Everything just seems fuzzy and strange.

As I finally leave the building, over an hour past the bell, I stop along the path to the gate and look up. I can see a waxing crescent moon in the sky, and something about it seems so enthralling.

Selena.

A strange feminine voice whispers sweetly in my mind, though no one is around. I pause.

As my eyes return to the earth, I spot something by the gate. At first glance I almost mistake it for a dog, but it's larger than any dog I've seen. The wolf's fur is as white as the snow itself, and she stares at me with crystal blue eyes. I look around for another person, if for nothing else than to simply confirm I'm not hallucinating, but there is no one around. Even beyond the school grounds, I hear no voices, no cars.

The wolf turns and wanders off, and I feel an intense compulsion to follow it. My feet move on their own before I can think better of it, and I follow the beast as it wanders through the suburban streets. All the while, I can't help but notice the city has become a ghost town. It's quiet, and there are no signs of life anywhere, as if everyone was whisked away except for me.

The wolf leads me to a street that hugs the perimeter of a large forest, and I follow her to a long, winding dirt driveway. At the driveway's end is a black-and-white gothic manor at the crest of a hill, with a small, frozen pond just out front. At the peak of the house is a large owl who seems to be staring straight into my very heart.

The wolf wanders up to the double doors, which open on their own for her. I follow her into the dark home with no hesitation.

My footsteps and the wolf's claws both echo as we stride across the hardwood floor, passing under the silver chandelier that decorates the foyer. The walls are navy and covered in oil paintings all bearing a lunar or winter motif, and the furniture is dark with lavender or royal blue upholstery. On either side of the room is a grand, L-shaped staircase leading up to a balcony on the second floor overlooking the room, and beneath is a long hall– one the wolf walks down, leaving me with no choice but to follow.

At the hall's end is a double door with the sigil of the full moon on it. I feel a sudden sharpness in my head. It doesn't hurt, per se, but more like a powerful shock. For a moment, I see a very large older man with a beard by the doors and the girl with ginger hair at my side. My hand flexes, and I can almost feel it grasping a strange, rectangular device.

As the doors open on their own the images disappear, and the wolf leads me onward.

I wander inside the room. A large two-story library stands before me with that same sigil painted on the floor, illuminated by the massive bay windows on the far side.

The room is full of fireflies, all paying no heed to the wolf or myself. They emit a silver glow, though, unlike any firefly I've seen. I am so distracted by them that I don't notice the other person in the room until the wolf wanders to their side and sits by them obediently.

They sit in a great blue armchair facing the windows, with a small, round table at the left side, holding only a black wood-bound book. A pale green moth sits atop the book, perfectly still, watching a thousand just like it flutter by outside the window. I stop at the edge of the sigil on the floor and watch the figure raise a pale hand to pet the wolf, affectionately scratching behind her ears for a moment. On her hand there are two rings—one identical to my own, the other a silver engagement ring with a round, blue diamond housed in a snowflake, with tiny white diamonds lining the top of the band.

She rises from her chair and steps around it to face me.

For a moment all I can do is stare, barely believing my eyes as my dreams and reality collide.

She has that same sparkling dress that fades from pale blue to dark blue, the same white fur cloak and large white hat.

The white-clad witch from my dreams.

Something tells me I have been waiting for this moment. Like I've been searching for it my whole life. I take a deep breath and muster up what little courage I can find in my heart, and I ask her:

"Who are you?"

II.
The White-Clad Witch

"The real question is 'who are you?', Moonchild."

I look back at her in silence for a moment before I decide how to respond. "My name is Lyra."

"Is it?" she replies, a subtle smirk across her face. "Time is a funny thing. The way it flows seems different for all of us, and often we are blissfully unaware of its cruel march forward. But all things that have life must eventually fade into memory, and all memories will one day be forgotten. From where I stand I am every bit as real as the life you've forgotten, but from where you stand, I am just an echo of the past."

"I don't know what any of that means." I study her with an intense expression but I can't seem to get a read on her. Everything about her makes me question whether she is even real, or if I'm in another dream. There is an invisible aura coming from her, a strange magnetic force that I can't help but find intriguing.

She raises her hand to me, and I feel lightheaded all of a sudden. I look down at my hands and I can see right through them. Though her lips are not moving I can hear her whispering *"don't panic"* in my ears, and the voice soothes my anxiety. Despite that, I can't help but think *'what is going on? What is happening?'*

I open my mouth to speak, but no noise escapes my mouth.

The sound of heavy footsteps fills the air like thunder, and then the man from my dream emerges from the door behind me. He walks right past me as if I am not even there, and something about his demeanor makes me nervous. He is familiar, somehow, and when I look at him I can almost recall a name from some deep, locked-away place in my mind.

The white-clad witch simply turns to him and coos, "My darling Seath."

The name awakens a different image of the man. He's older, with graying hair. His hair and beard are more wild, ungroomed, and he has a pot belly. There is something calmer, yet also sad, about this older version's demeanor.

"I sensed something in the air, and I saw that Yuki and Tsuki were restless," he says, all stern lines and harsh angles. "There is the presence of a second moon. Has Juniper–"

The witch raises her hand to silence him. "It is nothing to worry about, my love. I simply have an ethereal visitor." He turns back to look, his eyes scanning the room and passing right over me. I blink. "You will not be able to see her I'm afraid, for she is hiding in the shadows cast by my moon. But fear not, dear Seath, my guest and I are simply going to walk through the gardens. Would you kindly give us some privacy?"

Seath strides over to the witch, his expression softening, and ever-so-tenderly places his hands on her hips. She tilts the brim of her hat up and looks up at him, and for a moment the aura of mystery and fantasy about her is displaced, and she seems almost ordinary. Seath, too, gazes longingly at her, his hold on her delicate and gentle despite his size.

It's a little embarrassing to watch, but it's also hard to look away.

"Will you be okay?" he asks, his voice barely above a whisper.

In reply, she reaches her cool hand to his face and he closes his eyes at her touch. "Do not worry. She and I are kindred spirits. She is a Child of the Moon, like me," she tells him.

He opens his eyes and nods meaningfully, his eyes lingering on her for just a moment more before he parts and leaves the room. As the door closes, my body becomes tangible again.

The witch walks right up to me, and the book from the small table appears in her right hand and opens on its own. The whole world around me begins to blend into one single color, and only she remains in focus and unchanged. And then, as I blink, I find myself outside of the house, in a garden below the library's windows. Green moths surround us, thousands of them exploring the beautiful array of white, blue, lavender, and purple flowers.

Just beyond the garden is a tree-lined path that leads to a beautiful, serene lake behind the manor. As she starts to walk down the path, something connects in my mind.

"Yukiko!" I call. "Your name is Elatha Yukiko."

She turns back to look at me with a smile. "You remembered."

"Why do I know you?"

That impenetrable grin creeps across her face once more. "What you really want to know is why you can't stop dreaming about me."

She continues on down the path, and I feel a sense of frustration bubbling up inside my chest. It's like this is a game to her, and I'm getting tired of playing. I stomp down the path after her, catching up as she reaches the lake. I half expect to see some sort of cairn where she stands, but there is none.

"Tell me something. What do you remember of your past before this December?" she asks, gazing at the lake.

I pause, thinking for a moment. "Nothing, really."

"And can you remember what your parents look like? Or who your friends are?"

I shake my head and look out at the water, muttering, "No."

"Doesn't that strike you as odd?"

There is a certain irritating tone of cockiness in her voice as if she's in on some kind of secret. I can't tell if she's mocking me or not.

"A lot of things feel odd, or out of place."

"Is it the world around you that feels out of place, or is it you?" Yukiko probes. I frown. "Tell me, Moonchild, do you ever feel like you're living the wrong life?"

I look at my left hand. There is something at work here. It is like her words don't just reach my ears, but they call to something locked away in the deepest reaches of my mind. It is as if she is reaching inside me and trying to coax something out. But what?

"How can that be?" she presses, turning those knowing eyes towards me.

"This isn't my body," I answer instinctually, without even thinking. But that's—"But that's impossible!"

She turns to face me. "How many impossible things have you witnessed today?"

My head begins to pound with a crippling agony that brings tears to my eyes. I stumble away from her and become so dizzy that it makes me nauseous. I look at my left hand and see the cracks from my arm growing onto my hand. I can feel my heart thumping in my chest so hard that it might burst.

"What are you doing to me?" I choke out.

"Remember your name," she replies, ignoring my question.

"Lyra?" I say, but even before it escapes my lips I know that isn't right. Lyra is what this shell is called. My name . . . my *real* name . . .

"Wake from your dreams," she coos, her voice like a siren. "Say your name and awaken."

"Selena," I choke out.

A burst of memories fills my head. It's overwhelming at first, and the throbbing in my head brings me to my knees, but everything finally comes back to me.

I remember it all—Seath training me to use magic, Cara supporting me, Kiran coming to our school, Celly coming to life, and . . .

The panic sets in, and my heart races even faster. I keep gasping for air but I can't seem to find any. I just see her—the golden-eyed witch, Cyra Oralie, looking down on me in the field before the darkness swallows me whole.

Even as I find my breath, I can't stop hyperventilating.

"This isn't my body," I say, tears sliding down my face. "What happened to my body? What happened to Cara and Kiran? Where's Celly? What is this?"

Yukiko reaches her hand out and her sigil lights up briefly. The pain in my head subsides and my anxieties start to feel more manageable. Then I start to lose focus, everything becoming a calm, gentle blur, and I lose all strength in my legs. Just as I collapse, I find myself waking up again, shooting upright in bed.

Yukiko sits at the end of the large four-poster bed. Just from a quick glance at the bare room, I can tell I'm inside her manor once more.

"Look at your hand," she says finally, without bothering to face me.

I do. Sure enough, my sigil is back, though my hand is severely cracked, and I can even feel the cracks extending up my neck and to my left cheek.

"Who is she?" I ask quietly. "I mean, who am I? Like who does this body belong to? Sorry, this is all very confusing but I think you know what I'm trying to ask."

Yukiko nods. "Lyra is who you will become, should you give in to Cyra and surrender your power. She represents the mundane, safe life that awaits you if you give up magic. If you give up your powers, every day will be like the time you have spent in Lyra's form." She pauses, then asks, "Was it a bad life?"

I take a moment to think about the question. It wasn't, really. It was a calm, peaceful life. But it was also agonizingly boring. I felt like no matter what I did I could never accomplish anything meaningful—not because I lacked magical powers, but because I wasn't where I really belonged. It was a life without passion or hope.

Before I can give my verdict, Yukiko speaks up. "You can still choose that life if you want. Your story can end right here. Your fight with Cyra will end, and no one will come for you or bring harm to you for the rest of your days."

She might be right. But on the other hand, I can do good with magic. My power has brought me closer to Cara, introduced me to Kiran and Seath, and brought life to Celly. I was able to bring peace to Yukiko's thralls, and learn wonderful things from Seath I could use to help people.

"I don't want that," I say firmly. "I may have gotten this power from you, but it's mine now. I earned it, and I want to use it to do good. Cyra can't just take it from me."

Yukiko rises to her feet and offers me her hand. "It is time, then."

"Time for what?" I ask, taking her hand and climbing out of bed.

"To learn. I will tell you the true reason you can't hurt Cyra—the Sun's Curse."

III.

The Sun's Curse

I follow Yukiko through the upper halls of the manor. As we walk, a thought occurs to me.

"Am I really here, or is this just another dream?"

I can sense the smirk creeping across her face even with her back turned. "Two things can be true at the same time, Moonchild. I pulled your spirit out of time when you called to me and brought you here, but your true body is right where you left it, trapped in Cyra's spell."

My stomach twists at the thought.

As we reach the foyer and climb down the steps, she stops and watches the front door. It opens with a start, and the wolf enters. Yukiko holds out her right arm, and a great owl swoops in and lands on it. The owl is massive, and looks almost comical clinging to Yukiko's small frame.

The door to the library opens behind us, and the owl stretches her wings once more and soars down the hall, the wolf trailing behind her.

Yukiko looks back up at me as I cautiously descend the stairs. "Come along."

As I follow her I notice the owl and wolf have taken up the right and left ends of the sigil on the floor, and Yukiko herself stops at the far one. I hesitate as I reach the sigil. A green moth flutters just behind me.

If I take one more step, there will be no going back. I'll have to face Cyra again, and figure out how to beat her. Just thinking of her makes me shake—but my friends are waiting for me.

I look at Yukiko, who turns to face me, the sun peeking through the library window and casting her face in shadow.

I never noticed it before, but the presence of the moon is oppressive in her company. It feels like there are two moons—mine, and hers—and mine is being swallowed whole.

"Step forward, Selena Amaris, and I will teach you about the Sun's Curse, and about the powers of the moon," Yukiko instructs, lifting a hand towards me.

"But remember," she continues, "the choice is always yours. At any point you can go back and surrender to Cyra. You will lose your powers and forget everything to do with magic, but you will be allowed to live out a peaceful, safe life." Her gaze hardens. "The path now before you is not safe, but if you choose to follow it, you will accomplish great things."

I feel my lips purse. I can't just forget everything I've been through up to this point. My friends fought against Cyra for me, even though they never stood a chance. Their bravery is the only reason I even have this opportunity. I owe it to them to be brave now, to find a way to overcome Cyra and save them.

Taking a deep breath, I walk to the center of the sigil.

It lights up, a pale blue glow filling the room. The magic of the moon explodes around us, swallowing the room, the manor, and the whole world. I feel . . . incredible. I can begin to understand the true breadth of Yukiko's great power. She stands before me with a focused expression on her face.

Yukiko smiles, then begins; "The sun is the power of unrelenting, impenetrable light. It is an unstoppable force of brilliance. The moon shares the power of light, but it also holds within it the power of darkness."

The sun slowly disappears behind her, and everything goes dark. For a moment, I'm trapped again, lost in that darkness Cyra put me in. I feel my chest grow tight–

Gently, new lights begin to appear. I blink at what's before me. We're no longer in the library, but instead on top of a frozen lake covered in a thin dusting of snow that seems to go on forever, the only landmark in sight a single tree—a yew—emerging from a small island nearby. The sky is lit up with a spectacular array of northern lights and stars, and behind Yukiko is a frosty, pale full moon.

When I look over my shoulder, I can see a crescent moon in the opposite direction. I can't help but notice it looks so much smaller than hers.

Yukiko wanders over to the yew, where her familiars gather.

"There was a time when Cyra and I were partners," she says, looking up at her own moon. "We did everything together, and we understood each other so deeply, that it felt like no one else could ever possibly see me the way she did."

I recall what Mrs. Hoku said. It feels like a lifetime ago, now. *No one in this world loved Yukiko more than Seath Faolan, except maybe Cyra Oralie.*

"You two were lovers once, weren't you?" I ask.

Yukiko turns to me, a forlorn, pained expression on her face. She keeps her eyes up toward the stars, but I can't help but notice that her hand drifts to the crescent ring she wears. The ring we share. "That was a lifetime ago."

Her eyes drift to me, now clear of the past. She continues, "Cyra exploited her deep, intimate knowledge of me to cast a powerful curse. Curses are unlike any magic you've encountered thus far. They are extremely dangerous and difficult to perform, and even more difficult to get rid of. The Sun's Curse took the power of Cyra's entire coven combined—five experienced and talented witches—to cast. They bound my power to Cyra's so that I could not use my magic to defeat her." A rueful smile twists across her face. "And since you have succeeded my magic, and by extension my will, it would seem the curse has bound you to Cyra as well."

"So it's true that nothing I do can actually defeat her?" A shiver runs down my spine. Doesn't that mean it's hopeless to face her?

The green moth flutters down from the tree, and Yukiko receives it with her open palm. "Cyra's true power is her indomitable will. She is ferocious, and her spirit cannot be conquered. It's true that in a direct confrontation, you will never be able to overcome her. But once you fully embrace the power of the moon you will be able to evade her, and as your powers grow you will eventually find the way to break free of this curse."

"But I have embraced the moon!" I say back.

"Only that small sliver of it," she retorts, pointing to the crescent in the sky. As I turn to my own small moon, she is suddenly right at my back.

"Feel your moon. The whole moon, not just the crescent bathed in light, but the side wreathed in shadow as well," she whispers into my ear.

I raise my sigil hand toward my moon and focus on the magic that flows between us. The light is all I can sense for a long time, but as I close my eyes, I start to feel something else. There is something beyond the crescent, something I cannot see, but can still feel.

Something begins to stir inside me. I grit my teeth, my fear of Cyra being overcome by rage and frustration. The dark side of the moon does not provide comfort like the light side—it inspires anger and aggression. The more I reach for it, the more the cracks in my body spread.

Those feelings twist inside my chest, my hands balling into fists and my teeth grinding against each other. She hurt my friends. She robbed Kiran of his powers. She broke Cara's bow. She tormented Seath. She threw Celly. How dare she? How dare she tell me what I can do with my own magic!

I open my eyes and my sigil begins to glow brighter than ever. I raise my hand to the moon.

At first the shadows creep across the crescent, and the moon's light grows dull. I can feel every muscle in my body tense, and I feel hot, almost as if my skin is burning. I'm furious. I will break out of that evil monster's spell—and I'll hurt her for what she did to my friends.

I feel Yukiko's hand on my shoulder, but I violently shrug her away. "Back off!" I shout. "You're dead, this is my power now, not yours! You don't get to make decisions anymore!"

She grasps my shoulder once again and whispers in my ear, "Control the darkness, don't let it control you, my Moonchild."

Her words are hypnotic, and I can feel the influence of her own powerful moon over mine.

Gently, she says, "Remember what matters most of all."

I can see my friends in my mind, and my anger is met with concern. My desire to defeat Cyra contends with my desire to save them. And in the sky, the light side of the moon begins to fight back the shadows—and grow.

I must not let my anger control me . . . but I cannot suppress it either. Cyra must be defeated. But my friends must be protected first.

The moon responds to my will, transforming into a half-moon. Lyra's left arm crumbles and collapses, but my own remains in place in spirit form. I can feel Lyra's form collapsing around me, as if my spirit is shedding her body like a snake sheds its skin. I feel my connection to the broken mannequin that now lies at my feet slipping away.

The half-moon's power was too much for the doll—but it imbues me, and my sigil transforms. The lineart is gone, and the crescent symbol changes to a half-moon. It is surrounded by a solid ring. On either side of the main symbol, there are two orbs, one outlined, and one filled in.

The glow from my new sigil fades, and I collapse to my knees.

"What was that?" I say finally. "I was just so mad, I felt like I was going to explode. For a moment, I hated Cyra more than anything else."

"You embraced the dark," Yukiko says as if it's the simplest thing. "The darkness hides many things which we often would rather keep suppressed, and it can be frightening to tap into these things, but once you can control that which hides in the dark, you become exceptionally powerful."

She offers her hand, and I take it and rise to my feet.

"It is time, Moonchild," Yukiko says, a strange sense of mystery in her eyes. " The body of the doll can no longer sustain your spirit. Our souls do not do well in bodies they were not made for, after all. I can no longer keep you anchored here. Use your newfound powers to escape from the Witch of the Sun."

Suddenly everything around me begins to fade away, even Yukiko, leaving only my half-moon hanging alone in the dark.

"This will not be the last time we meet, Moonchild," Yukiko's voice echoes in the dark.

IV.

Half-Moon

I am alone in the void once more, and even my moon's light cannot penetrate the abyss. I can't even see my own hands. But this time, I'm not afraid.

I'm angry.

I gaze into my moon for a moment and think. How can I escape this abyss?

The sun is the power of unrelenting, impenetrable light.

Of course. Cyra can rob me of the light, but she cannot control the darkness. I can.

I bring my sigil hand to my heart, and the circle lights up. My whole body gives off a dull glow that the abyss cannot swallow. I clench my fist tightly, and within my chest I can feel my powers conquering the darkness around me. I feel the light build up inside, and I release it all at once with a powerful, blinding shockwave.

I find myself back on the athletic field at school, a cool winter breeze in the air. Cara and Celly lay near the bleachers to my right, Kiran is to my left, and Seath lies behind me. And ahead of me, engulfed in flame and levitating off the ground, is Cyra Oralie.

Her smirk turns to a glare as I stand defiantly before her.

She waves her hand in my direction and a great beam shoots down from the sun. On instinct I raise my hand, and a black fog appears in my palm, swallowing up the fire. As soon as her attack relents I look around.

I can feel that we are in another layer of alternate space. I can sense a weak point—perhaps a spot in magical space that was damaged by our fight earlier? If I can exploit it, I can make a door for us to escape. But how can I get everyone through?

As if on cue, I hear rustling and groaning behind me. *Seath.* From the corner of my eye, I can see Cara stirring as well, reaching out and wrapping her fingers around Celly.

If I can't pull this off, I won't be able to save everyone. I can't fail. I refuse.

"Your sigil," Cyra calls out. "It's different. What kind of trick is this?"

I smile. "There is no trick. I am Selena Amaris, the Witch of the Half-Moon, now, and I will not surrender my powers to you!"

At that moment the shadow of Cyra cast by the sun takes physical form as a large, ill-proportioned giant, who leaps at Cyra and traps her in a bear hug. At the same time, I shout out, "Seath, now!" and raise my hand to the empty space near Kiran's unconscious body.

As I focus with all my might, Seath forces himself to his feet and stumbles to Cara, slinging her over his shoulder. A tear opens in the world, acting as a portal out of the subspace. Seath and I run toward the tear, stopping only for him to gather Kiran up on his other shoulder. Just as we reach the tear, Cyra lets out an explosion of fire that destroys the shadow giant, and the last thing I see before I leap through the tear, is her glaring at me with hateful eyes.

Everything feels frantic, right from the second we emerge from the tear in space. It closes behind us, and Seath immediately runs for the wall of the school grounds. I race behind him, my heart pounding.

"Cyra created that subspace, so she can leave at will. We have seconds before she's on top of us," Seath shouts. "I can't climb the wall in my condition and it will take too long to get the others over top. Smash it!"

This isn't the time to ask questions—to think. I shut everything out of my mind except for escape and pry Celly from Cara's fingers.

"You're okay!" they say from behind the cracked screen. "How can I help?"

"My grimoire!" I say.

With Celly's power, the book appears in my hand, and I use the physical enhancement spell. Part of me wonders if this will work—but there's no time to think. We have to get away. Rather than letting the spell empower my entire body all at once, I condense all of the power into my left arm. As I reach the wall I step out in front of Seath, cock my arm back, and punch at the stone wall with all my might, releasing the spell at the same time.

It hurts—that's the first thing I notice before I even realize that my fist has completely sunken through the wall. The explosive force shatters the stone and creates a large hole.

I cry out in pain as I recoil my hand. It's bloodied and stinging, and frozen in a claw-like position. Moving it in any way hurts immensely, and I press it to my chest and clutch the wrist with my other hand as the pain drives tears from my eyes.

"Move it!" Seath barks. "We don't have time for pain."

Seath, Celly, and I run out into the street. At the same time a bronze hatchback a little ways ahead of us skids to a halt then reverses in our direction, stopping in the road just ahead of us. A familiar face bursts out of the passenger side door—I gape at Mrs. Hoku.

"Kiran!" she shouts, rushing over.

"He's fine, it's a long story! We need to get to Yukiko's manor immediately. Get the kids in the car," Seath orders. "Selena, sit up front, give them directions."

I drag myself to the passenger seat, struggling to get in as Mrs. Hoku sits in the back seat with Kiran and Cara, and Seath jumps in the boot.

"What happened?" Mr. Hoku asks as Celly levitates above the dash to give him directions.

"Cyra," I choke out. "She attacked us."

My eyes pop open wide, and I feel as though my heart weighs a thousand pounds. A feeling of dread causes the hairs on the back of my neck to tingle, and shivers run through every part of me.

"She's here," I say.

I look over my shoulder, and I can see Cyra's eagle familiar flying in a menacing circle before coming toward us. As we reach Owl Street, though, the eagle changes direction and veers north. I let out a sigh of relief.

"Mom?" I hear Kiran mutter, confused, before jerking fully conscious. "Selena!"

I look back and his eyes are locked on me. His hands are shaking. I can see tears of relief start to form in his brown eyes.

"Is everyone okay?" Cara croaks from beside him.

"Everyone's hurt," Seath says from the back. "But we're alive."

The car pulls into the driveway of the manor, stopping just short of the pond. Everyone slowly climbs out. Cara, upon exiting, stumbles to her knees, and Mr. Hoku gets down beside her before guiding her onto his back. Kiran leans against his mom as he walks, and Seath comes to my door and holds out his arms. I nod to him and he picks me up, carrying me toward the house.

"I know you didn't ask, but for the record, you're safe here," he says, his voice uncharacteristically soft. "Cyra won't set foot on the grounds here, the warding spells were made specifically to repel her."

But no matter what Seath says, I don't feel safe. He brings everyone up to the second story, and down the right-hand hallway to the room at the end. The room is dusty, but it's the same room I woke up in when I met Yukiko in the past, preserved exactly as I remember it.

The adults lay me on one side of the bed, Cara in the middle, and Kiran on the far side. Seath collapses against the wall on my side, sitting with his head in his hands . . . his blank hands.

My heart sinks. His sigil is completely gone. He spent the last of his power to help us. Maybe if I was stronger or more prepared . . .

Mrs. Hoku leaves and returns with her own worn, leather-bound grimoire, then heals our more major injuries, including my hand. The pain of my broken finger and knuckle bones repairing themselves is agonizing, but I'm too exhausted to even scream anymore. Even with the healing magic, my fingers feel stiff and awkward, and they crack with even the slightest movement.

It occurs to me that the overwhelming feeling of dread I sensed before is gone. I no longer feel the ominous and dominating power of the sun nearby.

"Cyra's gone," I whisper.

"She's just regrouping," Seath mutters. "This isn't over."

"But we survived," Cara says, sitting up in bed.

I turn over and see Kiran holding up his former sigil hand, now covered in a burn scar. He's staring at it. He sighs heavily and drops his hand. I wonder if he regrets fighting with us.

I want to say something to him, but can't fight off my exhaustion for a moment longer. The weight of my eyelids becomes unbearable, and I drift off to sleep.

When I wake back up, it's pitch black. I can feel Celly nearby, and as my eyes open their screen lights up, illuminating the room just a bit by extension. A crack runs down Celly's screen from top to bottom.

Kiran, his parents, and Seath are all gone. Cara is still sprawled out beside me, buried under the blankets. I wonder if she's okay? She must have been so scared before. I step out of bed and wander downstairs, using Celly to light my path.

I make my way to Yukiko's library, half-expecting to see her there, sitting in that armchair and gazing at the moon, but it's empty. The domineering force of her moon is gone, and the library feels lifeless and stale.

I wander back toward the foyer and open the front door. Seath is standing by the yew tree, his left hand against the trunk.

"Kiran moved to another room, but he's still here," he says, his gaze fixed on the dark sky. "His parents went home to pack up their things and get the dog. They'll be back soon."

I stand next to him, and he puts his arm around me.

"I saw Yukiko," I say finally. He looks down at me. "When it came down to just Cyra and I, she trapped me in this black void. I was so scared, and nobody could hear me or help me . . . I called for anyone to come and save me, but nobody answered—until I called Yukiko. She pulled my spirit back in time, thirty years ago, to meet her. She helped me evolve my sigil, and taught me to use the dark side of the moon to escape Cyra."

"I see," Seath says slowly. "So she was able to help you in the end."

"She told me things," I say, frowning. "She said I was bound by a curse, and that I could never defeat Cyra until I broke it." I look up at him. "I have to know, did you know about the curse?"

Seath lets out a heavy breath. "I knew she was cursed, but I didn't know if it would extend to you or not. I should have told you about it, I'm sorry," he says. "I'm sorry for a lot of things."

I hold out my hand, and Celly lands in my palm. I trace my finger along the crack. "Can you fix them?"

"Not anymore," he replies. "But I can show you how."

He reaches around the tree, taking a cane I hadn't noticed into his left hand. It's black and shiny, with a silver wolf head on the handle.

As we walk to the library I get the sense that he's trying his best not to lean on me. I'm certain he's more injured than he lets on, but I don't know how to confront him about it. His strides are short and slow, and I can't help but feel a sense of frailty in him that I have never seen before.

I feel that rage from before in my chest. A venomous voice echoes in my head, reminding me that Cyra did this.

But another part of me feels guilty. Maybe if I had trained harder, learned more, practiced more . . . maybe if I was smarter, or stronger, I could have protected everyone. Maybe nobody needed to get hurt.

Seath parts from me in the library and gestures for me to sit at the table. He looks around for a long time before finding a stained small brown book on a high shelf, barely big enough to fit into the palm of his hand. He sits beside me and thumbs through the hand-written pages, many of which are stained by messy hands.

"This belonged to a witch from the early 1900s, a woman Yukiko wished to mentor once, long ago. She had an interest in building and fixing old things, and developed many spells for working with one's hands," he says, sliding the book over to me open to a particular page.

I summon my grimoire and copy the circle he pointed out, then I lay Celly flat on the table. I invoke the circle and it glows in a soft orange hue, and sure enough, the cracks on Celly's screen slowly fade away. Celly's avatar appears much more vibrant and active, and they smile at me.

"Thank you," they say. The tone in their voice seems less synthetic and more natural than before. It's like Celly is becoming more 'alive' if that even makes any sense.

"What happened to her?" I ask Seath as I hand him the book back. "The witch, I mean."

Seath picked it up and looks at the cover for a while without saying anything. Finally, he let out a sigh. "Cyra killed her."

V.

Family

I stand on the balcony of a large clock tower, taller than the rest of the surrounding buildings in town, and it takes me a moment to realize where I am. City Hall. There is a plaza with a fountain at the building's entrance, and a mismatched two-story wing tacked onto the side. I always thought the modern architecture looked funny attached to this old building. I look back at the clock and find it frozen at the midnight position.

When I look up I startle—there's no sky. Instead, it's like a great calm sea is above the whole world, reflecting everything below.

I sense something in the distance, and sure enough, far away, on the rooftop of the school, I can just barely make out a strange figure. They are standing atop a magic circle, though I can't make out the details.

I can feel something dangerous stirring, and I notice ripples appearing in the sky-sea. A great shadow begins to move from within the reflection, and with a deafening crash a great monster bursts from the water.

The serpentine sea dragon, larger than any building in town, descends from the depths of the water, circling around the area above the school as it flies. The great monster stares at me with six massive, lidless eyes, each deep blue and cold.

The beast lets out a mighty bellow—

I jolt up in bed, and it takes me a minute to catch my breath.

Celly hovers around me. "Are you okay? You screamed in your sleep."

I nod. "It was another dream."

"Could it be prophetic?" they ask.

"It was," I say, still trying to get my lungs to cooperate. "But the dream was . . . weird. The sky was the sea and there was this huge monster, a black sea dragon as big as the lake behind the house."

"I wonder if we'll have to fight that, too," Cara whispers from beside me. She's turned away from me, hugging a pillow to her chest, and I catch a glimpse of tears on her cheek.

"I'm sorry, did I wake you up?" I ask, wondering if I should reach out or not.

She shakes her head. "I wasn't sleeping."

I wonder if she's anxious about today. Seath mentioned last night before I went back to bed that today he would be sitting down with all of our parents to discuss what happened with Cyra.

Still, I'm not sure what to say, and she lays quietly for a long time. Cara was never a morning person, though, and she did say she wasn't sleeping, so maybe she's just tired. I decide to give her some space and get up, heading for the shower with Celly.

In the antiquated bathroom next door, there is already a towel and some clothes laid out for me. Celly and I inspect the clothes for a moment—a vintage black dress with a white collar and ribbon belt tied in a bow at the back, and a white wool button-up cardigan.

I change into the dress after my shower and find that it fits surprisingly well. I wonder for a moment where it came from, until it occurs to me that it probably belonged to Yukiko. Come to think of it, we are about the same size, and she certainly wore other clothes, not just her blue dress and fur cloak that I've come to associate her with.

I step barefoot out of the bathroom, the wood floors cold against the soles of my feet. Celly comes to my hand and displays my texts for me. Mom and Dad blew up my phone when I didn't come home yesterday. Dozens of missed calls, almost a hundred missed text messages. Seeing the number of missed messages, I get a sense of weariness before I even open the conversations.

I don't have the energy to read through them all, but I do feel incredibly guilty. I should have called them, but everything was so crazy after the battle I didn't think of it.

I text my mom, asking her to bring some clothes from my room when she comes by today, and I quickly add another message that just says, *'I love you'*.

A new message quickly pops up, almost as if she is watching her phone, waiting for a message on the other end.

'I love you too, gummy bear. I'll bring some things over.'

"They must have been scared yesterday," Celly says. "I know I was."

"I'm going to apologize when I see them today for worrying them," I say, the guilt still sitting heavy on my chest. "And for other things, too."

I follow the sounds of furniture being moved around downstairs and find Seath and Kiran dragging in some extra chairs to the dining room. Seath is still using his cane, and every so often as he walks around his face screws up into a pained scowl, there and gone in less than a second. Maybe I could alleviate some of it with that healing spell I have, but I'm sure he wouldn't let me. Instead, I back up and sit at the bottom of the stairs by myself.

I can hear a car pull up outside, and Kiran's parents walk in with their dog, Sovanna. Mrs. Hoku does a double take of me when she enters, but I think nothing of it.

Perhaps she was just wondering where Cara is . . . or what I'm doing barefoot in the middle of winter.

The Hoku family breaks off to the kitchen, and shortly after another car pulls up. Cara's parents enter, and the familiar faces give me a sense of warmth.

Cara's mom is short and stout, with a wild explosion of ginger hair falling down almost to the small of her back. She's bundled in a dark green wool winter coat, and the man who follows has a short, messy beard, round glasses, and straight brown hair tied in a ponytail.

"Sweetie, are you okay?" her mom says as she comes to me, taking my face in her hands and looking me over.

I nod. "I broke my hand but it's better now. Mrs. Hoku healed it."

"Cara called us while you were sleeping," Mr. Philomena says. "I'm just glad you girls are safe. If you need anything, please don't hesitate. You're like a member of our family and we're here for you."

"Thank you," I say. "Cara's upstairs, if you want to see her. Make a right at the top, and it's the last room down the hall."

Another figure pokes their head around the door. A young boy of ten, with short, ruffled red hair and freckles and a face like Cara's stares back at me. It's been a long time since I've seen him, but that is most definitely Sean Philomena. He trails in behind his parents as they climb the stairs, looking back at me when he reaches the top.

My parents are the last to arrive. I jump to my feet as they come in weepy-eyed. Without a word my mom hugs me, and my dad kisses my head and brushes through my hair with his fingers. Mom's heartbeat is so soothing, and their embrace makes me feel so small and safe. Everything I'd been feeling up to that point, every moment since Cyra came after us where I've had to be strong, they all come flooding back now that I'm safe. The first tears escape my eyes, and then it's like the breaking of a dam—they stream ceaselessly down my face, and I sob into Mom's chest, clinging to her like I did when I was small.

Dad keeps stroking my hair, whispering into my ear, "You're okay baby girl, you're safe now."

I cry even harder. I cry and cry until no more tears will come, and my eyes are puffy and stinging.

Finally, I step back with a sniffle, and my dad hands me tissues to blow my nose and get cleaned up.

I've just barely managed to wipe the tears from my face when Seath steps into the foyer and says, "We're ready."

The families gather around the table, with Celly floating at my side.

Seath rests his elbows on the table and sighs. "We are here to discuss the events that happened yesterday, where the children's lives were in danger. I think we should start by explaining what exactly happened, so we're all on the same page," Seath says. "So, to start with, you all got a phone call from me the second I sensed the power of the sun appear in town. I warned you all that something dangerous was coming, and I ran to the school to try and protect the kids, but the fight had already started when I arrived. So, I think the best person to summarize what happened is Selena, as she is the only one who maintained consciousness the entire time."

I can feel everyone's eyes on me. It leaves me feeling self-conscious on top of my anxiety at reliving the experience. I try not to look at anyone else, just Seath, in the hopes that will help me focus.

"When school ended, things got really strange. The doors were locked and not even Kiran's magic could break us out. We were pulled into this–" I stutter trying to think of the word for it.

"Subspace," Kiran interrupts. "It's like a small chunk of the universe is pulled into this magical bubble where it becomes easier to manipulate reality and physics. Witches use subspaces sometimes to isolate magical people or beings from the real world, which is exactly what she did to us."

I nod. "Right, so everyone disappeared, and that woman, Cyra Oralie . . ." Both the memory and the mention of her name have my heart racing.

Mom and Dad both hold my hands, and I take a moment to collect myself before continuing. "She appeared. She tortured us, and she demanded that I give up my powers. Seath came to try and help, but she hurt him, too. I tried to fight back but she trapped me in some kind of black void where I was cut off from everyone. I tried calling for help, but nobody could hear me, and nobody answered. I was so scared, and I was alone . . . but when I called for Yukiko, something happened.”

“Go on,” Seath urges softly.

“I was brought back in time to when Yukiko was alive. She showed me some things and taught me how to use my powers better. Because of her, my sigil evolved,” I show the back of my hand to everyone, the half-moon almost glowing in the light. “And when she sent me back, I was able to use my new powers to distract Cyra and escape.”

“And here we are,” Seath concludes, leaning back in his chair.

My mom is the first to respond. “Why did this happen? What’s this attack about?”

“You all knew,” Cara says interjects. “Kiran, Seath, Mr. and Mrs. Hoku, you all knew who Cyra was, and none of you told us what she was capable of.”

“That’s not fair,” Kiran argues, his brow furrowed. “Nobody expected this to happen! I was caught off guard just as much as you were, and I shouldn’t have to tell you that out of all of us, I’m the one who lost everything!”

He shows us his burned hand with a scowl across his face. His mother gently taps his shoulder, and he relaxes. Mrs. Hoku looks guilty, not meeting anyone’s gaze and keeping her eyes low.

Cara turns her frustration to Seath. "From the beginning you've kept us in the dark, not just about Cyra, but about Yukiko, too. We could have been killed over these secrets, and that's not fair. If you were honest with us from the start, we might have made the informed decision not to study magic, but you wanted to pass on Yukiko's powers to Selena."

It seems Seath has little to say in his defense. He simply nods solemnly. He takes a deep breath and looks around the room, studying each and everyone's faces. "Long, long ago there was a woman with a talent for magic. She fashioned her own sigil, explored her power, and all on her own discovered other witches like herself. This woman never thought of herself as a warrior, and in the course of her life she rarely contemplated what use magic had in battle. She was a scholar, a researcher, an explorer, a scientist who studied magic, and most of all, she was a teacher. Her name was Venus, and she was the Witch of the Cosmos."

As Seath speaks, a streak of green catches my eye, and for a second I could swear I saw a butterfly in the room. I look around and it's gone, but in my mind, I can feel a strange sense of familiarity with Seath's story. The name Venus conjures the image of a woman with curly brown hair falling past her shoulders, a flowing ash-grey dress, a matching witch's hat, and a long raven-feathered cloak. There is something motherly and gentle about the woman's warm, toothy smile, though I don't know how I know her face.

"Venus traveled the world and sought young, gifted orphan girls to take into the protection of her magical orphanage and school. Her two most esteemed and powerful students were Cyra Oralie and Elatha Yukiko. The two were dedicated and ravenous apprentices, and before they were out of their teens they had already long-surpassed their mentor—and in time, they fell hopelessly in love with each other."

I see a flash of them together somewhere by the shore, young and carefree. Their usual air of mystery is nonexistent, and they look happy as they each steal glances of the other, holding hands and watching the sea. There is a vulnerability that I've never seen in either of them before.

"Things were peaceful, for a time," Seath continues. I can see the pity on his face, and something about it tells me this part of the story was a great source of pain for Yukiko. "But then there was a war in the magical community, and Venus was killed. Cyra and Yukiko fought together, but the war changed them, and they developed ideological differences. Cyra chose to begin policing magic, and trying to prevent future conflicts from happening, and Yukiko felt that she was becoming controlling. Yukiko fought to undermine Cyra, and their conflict spiraled out of control. By the time I met her, they had been locked in battle for sixty years."

"Cyra believed Yukiko was a trickster," Mrs. Hoku adds. "I think she attacked because she believes Selena's role as heir to Yukiko's powers is a part of some greater ploy to defeat her. And she isn't entirely wrong, is she Seath?"

Seath shakes his head. "I don't know what Yukiko intended when she passed her powers to Selena. By the end she felt trapped by the curse Cyra placed on her, and was desperate for a solution," Seath says. "What I do know is that Cyra intends to destroy Yukiko's legacy, and she believes Selena is a part of that legacy. I think after witnessing Selena's sigil evolve and push her back, Cyra will probably no longer accept her surrender. Yukiko is the only person Cyra ever feared, and I think that means she has marked Selena for death."

There is a short silence before the room descends into chaos. My parents and Cara's are furious, and our dads keep shouting over Seath, sometimes in tandem. Kiran slips off of his chair and makes a gesture with his head for me to follow. I nod and follow him toward the library with Cara behind us. I stand at the bay window with Celly, looking out toward the lake.

"What a mess," Cara says.

I turn and face them. I look at Kiran and gesture to his hand. "Do you regret it?"

He shakes his head. "Not a chance. I would do it again in a second."

"Maybe the two of you . . ." I trail off. It's hard to find the words, but everything that happened to them happened because of me. Cyra is after me. And by helping me, they put themselves at risk. Perhaps it would be better to go it alone. "Maybe we shouldn't be friends anymore. Cyra is going to keep coming after me, and if you two stay close, you could get hurt again."

"Don't say that," Cara says, voice cracking. "You can't just push us away. You have been my closest friend my whole life. How could you ask me to leave your side now, when things are hard? I'm not going anywhere."

"This is my fight, too," Kiran adds. "Cyra's other vassals are my friends—my brothers in arms. Cyra's actions dishonor them. Ilias, Augustus, Robin, Albert . . . I want to try and convince them to do the right thing and walk away from her."

"I'm not leaving either, Selena," Celly states. "I'm sorry I wasn't strong enough to fight by your side before, but next time I won't let Cyra keep me down."

A small smile creeps across my face. They are good friends.

It takes a long time for the yelling in the other room to subside, and things remain tense even as they quiet down. Eventually, the doors of the library open and Seath enters.

"We've come to a decision. Girls, you're gonna head back home to pack up your things. For now, you'll be living here," Seath says. "Kiran, you'd better go and talk to your parents for a bit."

He nods and walks out of the room quickly.

"What's going on?" I ask.

"Kiran's parents are going back to Florida to confront Cyra," Seath says. "They're going to try and reason with her. Kiran will be staying in my care until they get back."

VI.

Powerless

I turn over the black and green bracers in my hands and sigh. With everything that happened, Christmas came and went with very little fanfare. It was agreed to skip out on gift exchanges this year, but of course, Cara still gave everyone handmade gifts she'd made well in advance. The hand-knit purple scarf she made me is beautiful. It rests on the nightstand, and it has little gold crescent moon designs on each end.

If I had the money I'd get her a brand new bow. Instead, all I have are these bracers that I'm not even sure I should give her. Would she like them even though she doesn't have a bow? Or would they just be another reminder of everything that's gone wrong?

The smell of baked goods fills the air, shaking me out of my thoughts. I wander from the room and down the hall, chasing the smell, but stop at the top of the stairs. I look at the double doors there. Yukiko's bedroom.

Curiosity compels me to look, though I'm not sure if Seath would approve. I know he doesn't sleep in there—he almost always sleeps on the couch by the fireplace. He treats this place like a museum of Yukiko's life. There's something sad about that. I would think that after thirty years of living here alone, this place would feel more like her house than his, but it doesn't.

I take a deep breath and turn the handle of the left door.

The bedroom has an entryway with two other doors—one leading to the second floor of the library, and another leading to the actual master bathroom.

The bedroom is surprisingly . . . ordinary. A large four-poster bed with two dark nightstands rests against the wall on a raised platform. There is a dresser and an old-fashioned desk, an armchair with a side table and a reading lamp, and on the far end of the room next to the walk-in closet is a vanity desk. It's all very sterile. It seems to be the only room in the house Seath has actively dusted and maintained, so everything is well-preserved.

Something about the idea of Yukiko sitting down at her vanity and brushing her hair or applying makeup, being ordinary, seems to dispel some of the mystery around her. It makes her more human.

I walk over to the closet and open the door. Almost everything has been wrapped in plastic for protection, and it's hard to see what is inside. I don't know if I was expecting to see something ordinary, or a bunch of copies of her signature witch's outfit. Seeing everything preserved like this, though, is sad. Seath must have wrapped everything up himself. Something about the thought of him alone, in this room, trying to preserve every bit of Yukiko's identity in this closet, broke my heart—if only a little.

"Exploring?"

I turn to see Seath leaning against the entryway, cane in hand.

"I–I'm sorry," I stammer, pulling the closet door shut. "I was just curious, I guess."

"About what?"

I gesture around the room. "Her," I say. "I don't know, sometimes she feels like some elusive mystical figure, but then sometimes, like now, she seems so ordinary."

Seath shrugs. "So?"

"I guess it reminds me that I don't know anything about her. Everything I learn is just about her magic," I say.

Seath pauses for a moment. I'm not really sure he's going to say anything at all, then–

"She liked mischief. She would create ice chips and put them down my clothes sometimes for a laugh," he says, a grin creeping across his face.

I can't help but smile. "I can't imagine her like that."

"She had a wonderful laugh. It was always hard to be mad at her for her little pranks when she was laughing like that," Seath says. "When she was alive, I found it nice, in a way, that she was only her true self with me. It was like this special, beautiful thing that I got to have all to myself. But now, I wish I could have shared that side of her with the world. Nobody remembers her like I do."

There is a brief silence, then Seath gestures for me to exit. He follows me out of the room, and as we leave, he extends his hand through the open air to the door, but nothing happens.

He lets out a sigh and physically walks back to close the door by hand.

We part ways at the bottom of the stairs. I watch as he disappears down the hall to the library, passing Kiran's dog, Sovanna, as she sleeps sprawled out on the floor. I had almost forgotten his parents left her here, too.

I head to the kitchen where Kiran, Celly, and Cara are, if the sounds coming from there are any indication. A plate of warm, fresh muffins sits on the kitchen island, next to a loaf of banana bread and a pitcher full of some sort of fruit smoothie.

"You two made food again?" I ask as I wander in.

"Of course," Cara groans as she sips her coffee and leans against the counter. "I am certain Seath would starve to death without us. If we don't make anything then there's no food around here."

"What did he do before we moved in?" I ask.

"Spend a frankly embarrassing amount of money on takeaway, probably" Kiran replies glibly.

"I think he's single-handedly responsible for keeping Luigi's pizza in business," Cara jokes.

Celly flies over to me. "Did you sleep well, Selena?"

"Yeah," I lie, forcing a smile. It's been hard to get comfortable here in this house. I've never spent this long away from my parents.

Seath comes in, meandering over to the island to take a muffin. He finishes the entire thing in three bites before tearing off a chunk of the banana bread and eating that, too. I can feel Cara's disappointment from here.

"Manners!" she says with a huff. "Were you raised by wild animals?"

"For the record, I survived just fine before you kids moved in and started making a mess of my kitchen," Seath declares.

"Yeah, survived on pizza and burgers," Kiran mutters under his breath.

"I heard that, brat," he replies, wandering out of the room. "Come out to the lake, I have something for you kids."

I look back at the others, all of whom seem intrigued. We, along with Sovanna, follow Seath out through the side door between the kitchen and the walk-in pantry and follow the path to the garden and out to the lake. I can't help but notice as we reach the soft earth of the lake shore that Seath seems to struggle with his cane. It keeps getting stuck in the mud.

He walks over to a tree just off of the shore and retrieves a smooth, snow-white bow and a quiver full of arrows.

"Miss Cara, this is for you," he says, as she runs up to him. At first she seems giddy, almost swept up in the excitement of receiving a gift, but as she gets close to him I can see her smile drop and her posture change.

She slings the quiver over her shoulder and takes the bow into her hands with an aura of reverence, as if accepting the gift comes with some heavy weight upon her shoulders. The bow is different from the one she had before—while strung, this one makes a perfect D shape. "It's a classic English longbow," she says. "This is beautiful. Thank you."

"As for Mister Sassy-Commentary over there," Seath mocks, retrieving a sword from the same hidden spot. "Now that you've lost your powers, you might find it useful to train with something like this. You might not be able to do magic anymore, but the girls can enchant this for you."

Kiran takes it and removes it from the sheath. The blade is probably about three feet, and there is an owl face on either side of the pommel. It looks old and heavy. Kiran runs his hand along the flat of the blade, acquainting himself with the steel. It suits him—he does seem the type who would make a good knight. He studies it with a keen interest.

"These belonged to Yukiko," Seath says. "She kept a small collection of armaments. I'm sharing them with you in the hopes that you'll develop your skills, and be better able to protect yourself."

"Funny," Kiran says, giving the sword a couple of test swings through the air. "I would have figured she'd have katanas."

"That assumption is a bit problematic," Cara says.

"For the record," Seath says. "Yukiko does have two katanas, a wakizashi, and a naginata. She also has a claymore, a zweihander, a labrys, twin khopeshes, a japanese longbow, a mongolian horsebow, two crossbows, a blunderbuss that does not work, and an ivory-handled flintlock pistol."

"What's a labrys?" I ask, though, really, that's only the first of many questions I have.

"A labrys is a double-bitted axe, according to Greek Middle-Platonist Philosopher Plutarch," Celly explains.

Seath gestures a little ways down the shore where two archery targets have been set up. Cara nods, getting the picture, and she walks off, talking her grimoire out to practice spells and shooting. He then finally retrieves his own grimoire, and hands it to me.

I frown. "Wha–"

"I can't use it anymore," he explains. "But you can. I've been annotating it all week. There are hundreds of spells in here, and I want you to study and learn them. Meditate using your powers and try to commune with the moon, that's what Yukiko did. It helped her figure things out."

I nod, taking the book from his hands. It feels melancholic, almost. It's sad to see him give it up like this. This isn't just a book, this is his life story. His history with Yukiko, learning magic at her side. It feels wrong that I should have it, but I also feel lucky to have this opportunity to study it.

"As for you, boy," Seath says to Kiran as his lips curl into a grin. "You and I are going to practice your sword skills."

Seath grips the shaft of the cane just below the handle and twists it, allowing him to pull a hidden blade free from within.

I back away, finding a tree to sit against that gives me a good view of both Kiran and Cara's training. Sovanna flops down nearby, and I absent-mindedly pet her. Celly summons my grimoire for me, and I set it aside and open Seath's. Even just flipping through the pages, I can tell there is a treasure trove of information within.

In the early pages, it seems Seath started learning similarly to Cara and I. His grimoire is much more organized—there are tabs and sections, unlike mine, where there is no rhyme or reason. I copy over a few spells I recognize, like the one he used to make Kiran promise not to betray our trust, and the one he used to read my dreams. There are others, too, like more elaborate healing spells, which I start copying over next.

In my reading, I find an interesting spell. The notes read:

The Fairy Spell: for flying

The circle features what looks like a butterfly in the center. I make a point of copying that one over next, and contemplating what, exactly, 'for flying' could mean. Perhaps it will give me wings?

I take a break from my reading to observe the others.

Cara is practicing imbuing her arrows. She fires one, and on impact it releases crystal shards in every direction. Everything the shards hit gets coated in a sheet of ice. She then fires another one that liquifies the arrow into a sickly green color. As the goo splatters on the other target it spreads and melts everything it touches like acid.

Kiran, on the other hand, can't seem to beat Seath as they spar.

"There's something off about Kiran's movements," I say finally.

"I believe Kiran has been using magic to enhance his hand-eye coordination, strength, and agility. Without his sigil, it appears that he is struggling to fight at the same level," Celly responds.

"It's not just him." I saw Seath's speed and strength firsthand when we were hunting thralls. His experience is carrying him, but he seems much slower now, and much more frail. His knees seem stiff, and he's showing lines and wrinkles in his face I never noticed before. There's a dullness in his eyes, and his hair seems to be thinning and losing its luster.

I try to remind myself that it's normal. He is over sixty, after all, it's probably not that unusual for his age to start catching up to him after something as traumatic as the fight with Cyra. Still, it worries me to see him declining right before my eyes.

With a sigh, I return my attention to his grimoire.

VII.
Auld Lang Syne

After our extensive training, Cara and Kiran make everyone tomato soup and vegan grilled cheese sandwiches. I look at mine, and back at her, and I just think for a moment, *I really miss cheese, chicken, and bacon*. I feel a little guilty because she went out of her way to prepare food for everyone, and part of me is glad it wasn't left to Seath who'd just get takeout or frozen food every day, but also eating nothing but vegan food is making me long for my dad's cooking.

Kiran leans back on the couch with a sigh. "You know what this needs?"

Is he talking about the food? Please say what I'm thinking for me.

"What?" Cara asks innocently.

"A TV. How is there not a single TV in this entire house?"

I look down at my sandwich in defeat. *You were my last hope, Kiran.*

"You're joking, right?" Seath chimes in. "Look in the room behind you."

Kiran gets up and walks to the door behind his couch, and I follow him, curious. He opens the door and reveals a lounge area with a bar, a radio, and an admittedly impressive sound system on the far wall near a little alcove.

"It's just a bar," Kiran replies.

Seath walks past us, and gestures to the alcove, which upon further inspection is hiding a set of stairs leading to the basement. "Downstairs."

We all clamor down the stairs and find ourselves in a large home theater with leather couches that all have cupholders and reclining seats.

"You mean you were hiding this the whole time?" Kiran shouts.

"We could watch the new years countdown on this tonight!" Cara squeals. "And here I was thinking we weren't going to do anything to celebrate!"

"We should dress up nice," Kiran suggests. "Like, really nice, make a formal kind of party of it."

"How formal?" I ask.

"Like, new-years-gala formal," he replies. His eyes drop for a moment, and he looks like he's lost in a sad thought. "Every New Year's Eve, Cyra hosts a formal gala, it's supposed to be for charity but really it's for getting witches all around the world together. When I was a little kid, before I became her vassal, Cyra taught me how to dance."

"I can't imagine her doing that," Cara says.

"It was important to her that we could do things like that with confidence. She was very big on appearances. She said 'the sun must shine brightest so the people in darkness can have warmth.'" His face drops, as if the memory is tainted by their recent falling out.

Seath puts a hand on Kiran's shoulder. "Cyra has always been tough on her friends and fierce to her enemies. If she believes in you she won't accept failure. I bet she expected the world of you."

He nods in reply. "Yeah, she was tough, but she was also patient and strong."

Kiran always speaks so highly of her. It must hurt to go against her. I wish I knew what to say in this situation to make him feel better. There is a heavy silence that hangs in the air.

"Okay," Cara says. "Let's do it. Let's do the party. I think it's a nice tradition."

Throwing together a formal evening with no notice is easier said than done, so both Cara and I end up texting our parents for help. At least Kiran has a suit here already. Still, as Cara waits in the foyer for her mom, I figure now is a good time to give her my Christmas gift.

I run up to grab the bracers, then head back down, holding them behind my back as I approach her.

She turns away from the window and looks at me suspiciously. "You have something, don't you?"

I grin from ear to ear. "Maybe," I reply playfully, leaning on the 'ay' sound.

I show her the bracers, presenting them unwrapped. "I got them before everything happened, but then your bow was broken and I didn't want to make you sad, but since Seath gave you Yukiko's bow–"

She throws her arms around me in a giddy hug, squealing, "Thank you!"

She takes them from my hands and tries them on—a perfect, snug fit. I've seen the bruises whiplash from her bowstring can cause, so this should help a lot. "Thank you, these are perfect. I always wanted something like this!"

Her mom arrives, and Cara disappears to her room to get ready. My mom comes shortly after and insists on helping me get ready, though I think it's more for her benefit than for mine. The dress is lovely—I wore it once to a wedding, and I'm grateful it still fits even if it is a little snug. The midnight purple gown reaches my ankles, and the bodice is decorated with sparkly, flowery, lavender lace patterns extending down to my right hip. I pin the brooch Kiran gave me to the front, and Mom does my hair in front of the bathroom mirror, twisting it into a crown braid with soft curls down my back.

When she's finished, she spins me around on my heels and looks me up and down. "Oh honey, you look perfect."

"Moooommm," I say as she fusses over me. "You're only saying that because you're supposed to."

"True, but just because I should say something positive doesn't mean I don't mean it," she replies, getting ready to apply a bit of makeup to my face. She snaps at me to stay still at every minor motion I make, and even though I find it annoying, I also can't help but smile. She has Celly take plenty of photos, then she escorts me back down to the foyer, where Seath is waiting in a handsome black-on-black suit with his hair tied back and his beard trimmed.

He watches me with a warm smile. "You clean up nice, kid."

"You don't look so bad yourself," Mom replies. "What a difference a simple comb and nice clothes make!"

"Mrs. Amaris, you're going to make me blush," he replies playfully.

"I didn't know dogs could do that," Kiran calls from the top of the stairs, a sly smirk on his face.

Speaking of cleaning up nice, I can't help but stare for a moment. With his hair brushed back and his steel grey suit and purple shirt, he looks really handsome.

I turn to mom, trying to manually change my focus and break my stare. "So are you going home now?" I blurt out.

Her eyes flick between myself and Kiran for a moment, and the half-grin that forms on her lips makes me want to scream. I can see that look—don't make assumptions, Mom!

"I'm going to hang around for a bit and talk to Seath, if that's okay," she says. "Why don't you head downstairs with your *friend*?"

Just that teasing emphasis makes my cheeks feel hot, and I know I'm blushing despite trying not to.

As we turn to head out, I hear hurried steps from the second floor, and Cara appears at the top of the stairs next in her flowery emerald green ballgown. With her hair in a braided updo and her sheer sleeves and glittery eye-shadow, she looks like a fairy princess.

"Wait for me!" she calls as she hurries down the stairs as fast as her heels will carry her.

"Miss Cara," Seath says. "I don't have any words that will suffice, so you'll have to settle for 'wow'."

"Thank you," she replies.

Cara catches up to Kiran and I. "You two are matching! If I knew I would have looked for something purple, too." She turns to me, fussing with my skirt, then hers. "Selena! You look so cute! How do I look? Is this too much?"

"You're beautiful," I reply. I can see Kiran nodding along in agreement from the corner of my eye.

The three of us head down to the basement and Cara puts on some music with her phone, playing it through the house speakers. It's a little embarrassing at first, but Cara starts dancing and won't give me a chance to sit. Through sheer force of will she compels both Kiran and I to dance with her. Eventually, the commotion causes Sovanna to come running, and the dog watches us, tail wagging wildly. Even Celly joins us, their avatar dancing on screen as they levitate around, snapping all kinds of photos.

We take a break from dancing for dinner—Italian takeout provided by Seath, who keeps to himself at the back of the room, slowly sipping a big glass of amber liquor. His eyes keep flicking back and forth between Kiran and I for some reason, narrowing as time goes on. As a slow song starts, he sets his glass and cane down and offers his hand to Cara. "May I have this dance?"

As Cara accepts, I can see him slyly kicking Kiran's leg. Kiran shoots up to his feet, his cheeks slightly flushed, and he walks over to me. He holds his hand out to me, but he won't make eye contact. I can't help but notice that his hand is ever-so-slightly shaky, and perhaps a little clammy.

I can feel my heart race as I reach out my hand, and I hesitate for a moment before placing it in his. A dorky smile fills his face as he pulls me to my feet.

He's a good dancer, leading with ease. After stepping on his feet twice in a row, I conclude that I, on the other hand, am not.

"I'm sorry," I say as the urge to flee in embarrassment grows.

He just shakes his head with that same cool smile. "Just take a deep breath and slow down. Follow my lead, okay?"

I do as he says, taking a big breath. In just a few moments my embarrassment is forgotten, and I'm able to relax.

For the next song, Seath and Kiran switch partners. I feel like a toy dancing with Seath—he towers over me, and I feel so tiny next to him.

"I used to dance with Yukiko back when she was still alive. We would go somewhere high up and watch the fireworks," Seath says wistfully. "I'd sing to her at the end of the night, and she loved it."

"You could sing tonight," Celly says. I nod. I'd love to hear that.

He simply shrugs in reply, stepping away with a bow as the song ends. He collects his drink and cane and wanders back upstairs, letting us get back to our party.

As the time grows closer to midnight we tune into a livestream of the New York City ball drop, our energy almost completely expired. My feet are sore from dancing for so long, and I rest, leaned back on one of the couches, with a water bottle and Sovanna for company. Only Celly remains infinitely energetic.

The four of us loudly join in the final countdown, *wooing* as we usher in the New Year.

As we climb up the stairs, ready to call it a night, I notice Seath outside from the foyer window. I quietly motion for Kiran, Celly, and Cara to follow me as I open the front door and peak outside.

He stands by the yew tree with his hand on the trunk as he sings beautifully into the night.

> *Should old acquaintance be forgot,*
> *and never brought to mind?*
> *Should old acquaintance be forgot,*
> *and auld lang syne?*
>
> *For auld lang syne, my dear,*
> *for auld lang syne,*
> *we'll take a cup of kindness yet,*
> *for auld lang syne.*
>
> *And surely you'll buy your pint cup!*
> *and surely I'll buy mine!*
> *And we'll take a cup o' kindness yet,*
> *for auld lang syne.*
>
> *For auld lang syne, my dear,*
> *for auld lang syne,*
> *we'll take a cup of kindness yet,*
> *for auld lang syne.*

There is a haunting sense of sorrow as his voice echoes into the starlit sky, and I can't help but wonder if it will reach Yukiko, wherever she may be.

VIII.

Homeroom

It's a strange feeling getting ready in the morning to head back to school. The last time I was there, Cyra attacked. As I prepare to trudge through the freshly fallen snow with Kiran and Cara, this sense of anxiety fills my stomach with dread.

I fidget with my new scarf while waiting for the others to finish getting ready.

Celly slips from my pocket and levitates in front of me. "What's wrong?"

"It was so easy for Cyra to get to us, and now we're just going back. What if she attacks again?" I take my grimoire from the coffee table and cast the sense-expanding spell for the third time that morning, searching for any trace of the presence of the sun, but I detect nothing.

"Seath assured us that she wouldn't try attacking us again at school since we can always just run back to the house," Celly says. "It will be okay. We'll be ready to defend ourselves when she does come back."

"But she'll be ready, too," I retort, looking down at my shaking hands.

Celly lowers themselves to stay in my field of view, and they reach out toward the screen. "The first time I have ever felt fear was when Cyra cracked my screen. I understand how powerful that feeling is now. I might not be able to make it go away, but I'll be right here with you, even if she does come back."

Before I can say anything I hear footsteps coming down the stairs, and Cara comes around the corner with her grimoire, Kiran following closely behind.

I can see two pins pierced into the cover that weren't there before—a bow and a sword, both placed in the bottom right corner.

"Selena, guess what?" Kiran asks with a proud smile.

"What?"

"Cara and I were in the library after you went to bed, and we found this book all about using magic to change or transform objects or bind them," Kiran says, then he nudged Cara with his elbow. "So she started experimenting, and look!"

Cara holds up her grimoire and gestures to the pins, explaining, "I used some of the cutlery as alchemic material for the pins, and bound the sword and bow to them. So now—"Cara snaps her fingers and the bow pin transforms into Yukiko's bow, and with another snap it returns to its pin form on the cover. "It's too tricky to do the arrows just yet because if I do the whole bundle then they can't return to their small form if I'm missing any, and if I do them individually then it's a big mess and honestly Seath doesn't own that many spoons," Cara explains, grinning. "But I'll learn eventually!"

"That's really cool! You'll have to teach me how to do that." I say with a forced smile. I really am proud of her, but at the same time it's hard to muster enthusiasm when that feeling of dread continues to fester in the pit of my stomach.

Seeing them put on a brave face is comforting, but it doesn't make the anxiety in my heart go away. As we put on our shoes and begin our walk to school, that feeling only gets worse.

As the school gate comes into view, I can feel my heart start to race. The distressed thumping feels so loud it drowns out all other noise, and I start to slow my stride, falling a bit behind Kiran and Cara.

The school gate feels like the maw of a great beast just waiting for me to throw myself down its gaping gullet. My feet start to feel like lead weights, and I stop just short of the gate. There's something wrong with my breathing. I step away from the gate and lean against the wall for support, trying to draw in as much air as I can, but no matter what I do I can't breathe. I keep seeing her face in my mind, and it's clearer to me than Cara and Kiran, who are both holding on to me. I keep looking around. Something is wrong. Is this her? Is this a spell? Is she here? What's happening?

I can't breathe. I need to get away, I need to run somewhere—anywhere. I can't be here. She's coming for me. She–

"Focus!" a sharp, feminine voice commands. "Look around you. What do you see?"

Everything feels like it's spinning, but I try to focus on one thing at a time, scanning my surroundings.

"Out loud! What do you see?" the voice demands.

"Snow, uhh footprints . . . trees on the boulevard . . ." It's so hard to stay focused, but I just force myself to go from one thing to the next. "There are houses . . . that one has a red door. There's cars over in the parking lot, I think that Honda is the Principal's car . . ."

"What's your name, honey?"

"Selena . . . I'm Selena."

"Take a few deep breaths Selena," the stranger says. I do as she says, trying and failing, then managing to get a proper breath. Then another. "How do you feel now?"

My heart is still pounding, but I can breathe. My mind isn't racing anymore, I feel– "Better."

I finally take a look at the thin, blue-eyed stranger. She has big dimples and a mole just below her right eye. She looks sophisticated and proper.

Cara steps up beside me, linking her arm in mine. "I'm Cara," she says. "Are you a teacher here?"

The woman adjusts her big round glasses for a moment, revealing a silver ring with a single diamond and several sea-green stones along the band on her finger. "Yes. I'm new here, actually. My name is Ms. Rivers." Her gaze swings to Kiran. "And I didn't catch your name, young man?"

"Kiran," he replies, crossing his arms.

Ms. Rivers nods, then looks back at me and says, "Selena, that was quite a panic attack. Do you want to sit down for a bit, or maybe go home? I can escort you to the office."

A panic attack? I thought my heart was going to explode, or that I would suffocate. I was sure that it had to be some sort of terrible magic attack, not . . . I shake my head. "I'm okay now."

"At least let me walk you inside," Ms. Rivers says with a warm smile.

She has impeccable posture as she walks. With her hair in a tight bun and her white blouse kept immaculate, she seems very prim and proper. There's something incredibly charming about her, though I can't exactly place what it is. She just seems warm and compassionate.

As we enter the doors, held open for us by Kiran, Ms. Rivers stops us.

"I suppose this is where I leave you. Are you sure you're feeling better, Selena?" she asks. "There's no shame in taking a mental health day, you know. The school will still be here tomorrow."

I nod and smile back at her. "I feel a lot better now, thank you."

She smiles at us then walks down the hall. We watch her go for a moment before we turn and head to our own lockers.

"Selena, do you know what set you off?" Cara asks as the three of us reach my locker.

I shrug. "I've been anxious about Cyra all morning. This is where everything happened, so to be back here . . . I guess I got overwhelmed."

"I'm sorry," Cara says. "If you want I can skip club activities and walk home with you today?"

"It's okay, really, I'm good. Ms. Rivers helped a lot, and Kiran will be walking home with me, right?" I say, looking at him. He nods. "So it'll be okay."

After gathering our things, we all head off to homeroom, taking up our seats in class. Just before the bell rings, the principal—a stout, dark, older man with a crown of grey hair atop his head—walks in with Ms. Rivers at his side. He leans against the teacher's desk and fiddles with his tan suit sleeves as he waits through the morning announcements to finish over the loud speaker. Finally, at their conclusion, he stands tall and claps his hand once to get everyone's attention.

"Listen up class," he says. "I know you were all expecting Mr. Gallardo this semester, however, he had a family emergency and will be taking a sabbatical for the foreseeable future. Ms. Rivers here has graciously offered to fill in for him for as long as need be, so please give her a warm welcome and treat her with the utmost respect."

Ms. Rivers does a playful curtsy and addresses the class. "It is wonderful to meet you all. I look forward to getting to know all of you, as well as this lovely town. Let's all have a good semester together!"

I let out a long breath. Despite all the trouble last year, this semester is off to a good start.

IX.

Doppleganger

Being home feels great, especially after spending weeks cooped up at Yukiko's manor. Dad made a big seafood medley, and Mom took me shopping to end the second week of school on a high note. Following that incredible dinner, I find myself on the couch with Mom, playing a sword game with her on the TV while Dad cheers us on.

We play well past sunset, until Mom finally sets her controller down and stretches. "I can't tell you how much I missed doing this, Gummybear!"

I let a small smile creep across my face. "We made a lot of progress."

"More so than I made with Daddy, he's terrible at this," Mom quips.

Dad laughs. "Ah, I can't get into these things, they make them way too complicated these days. I'd rather watch, anyways. I like the stories."

"And you hate losing," Mom retorts.

"This is the kind of merciless teasing I had to endure before you started filling in as her player two," he says to me in mock exasperation.

There is a pause in the air, and Mom and Dad exchange a look and a nod. They're definitely up to something. Mom then turns to me and pats my knee. "I have something to show you before you go."

I watch as she stands up, walks over to the TV stand, and opens a drawer there. She takes out a white hardcover journal with gold trim and brings it to me. There is a familiar sense to the book as I take it into my hands.

But it couldn't be . . .

I open it up and sure enough, right there on the first page, is the spell for copying magic circles, followed by the all-to-familiar plant spell.

"Seath is teaching you?" I ask, looking back at her. She nods.

"We couldn't protect you from that woman, and right now we can't even keep you here, in our home," Dad says, his fists clenched in his lap. "It's so frustrating, knowing that there isn't much we can do to help you."

"Dad . . ."

Mom takes the book back. "I'm studying wards and other types of protective spells. I want to be able to make this house safe again, so you can come home."

I don't know what to say. As much as I missed home, I guess I never thought about how this has been affecting them as well. I search for the words, wondering what I could possibly say. Maybe I need to apologize. Maybe I need to get better with my magic—so I can be strong enough that they don't have to worry.

Mom and Dad sit on either side of me, and they both hug me tightly, and it feels so warm. They're trying their best, so I need to keep practicing my magical talents, too, and figure out how to beat Cyra's curse.

"We love you so much, Gummybear," Mom says.

"I love you both, too," I reply quietly.

After a little while we say goodnight and I start walking back to Yukiko's manor. It's not a long walk, though it is chilly out.

As I get halfway there, I get the uncomfortable sensation that I'm being watched. I can feel a strangeness in the air, but I can't quite place this presence. It's different from both the sun and the moon. If anything, it reminds me of the sea dragon I saw in my dreams.

Just then I hear an eerie, feminine giggle from behind me. I spin on my heel, heart pounding, but there's nothing there. I take Celly from my pocket and wake them up as I back slowly into the street.

"What is it, Selena?" they ask, floating near me.

Another giggle from behind sends a chill down my spine. "I sense strange magic, Celly."

"That's an interesting toy," the voice calls. "Can I play with it?"

As I whip around I finally see the source of the magical presence, and I would scream if not for my voice and breath getting caught in my throat. An apparition wearing my own face stares at me, her lips stretching unnaturally across her face, almost to her ears, and curled up in a grotesque grin. Everything about her, from her witch's garb to her very skin, looks like she is made of glass.

"What are you?" I shout, raising my sigil hand.

She just stares back at me. "Big sister Cyra is not very happy you defied her. She tried to settle this without anyone else having to die, but you turned her down." As she speaks her too-wide smile shows all her jagged, crooked teeth. "So now I get to play!"

As the apparition talks, air bubbles form in her mouth and throat. My stomach drops. She's not made of glass—she's made of water.

Whatever this creature is, she works for Cyra. What should I do? Try to run for the manor? I doubt she would have ambushed me if she thought I could just run away. On the other hand, I have no idea what I'm getting myself into.

"Celly, call Seath," I say, but they stare back at the apparition, wide-eyed. "Celly?"

"I can't," they reply. "She's interfering with my signal!"

I summon my grimoire to my hand. If I can't run or call for help, then the only thing I can do is fight. I launch a fire spell directly at her, but the impact is absorbed, doing nothing but create air bubbles through her body.

The apparition raises her left hand toward me. "My turn."

A bolt of fire flies at me faster than I can react. I feel a blunt jab to my stomach that knocks me back. The stench of singed fabric reaches my nose, and I have to suppress the urge to vomit from the impact.

Celly starts flinging lightning bolts at her, but water-me keeps avoiding them as she walks closer, that deranged expression locked on me.

I drag myself to my feet. I need to think of something, I can't let that thing get close to me. Every step she takes fills me with dread and I can feel my legs shaking. Everything inside me screams *stay away*.Her hand rapidly extends at me, closing the distance and turning into a bubble that engulfs my head.

I try to pull it off, but my fingers slip right through the chilled water. I can't breathe. I need to get it off. I need to get away. I start choking, gagging on the water. My eyes sting, yet I dare not close them, I keep searching for anything I can use to escape.

For a moment, through the water, I can see a silhouette, but my vision is too blurred to make it out.

I frantically claw at the bubble, even scratching my own skin in the process, but there's nothing to grip. I feel the water slide through my fingers and snake down my throat. Each involuntary attempt to breathe only draws more water into my lungs.

My knees weaken and I crash to the ground, the sound of the creature's shrill, maniacal laughter echoing around me.

There is a thunderous crash, and all at once the connection is broken and the water bubble collapses. I fall to my knees and immediately break into a coughing fit until I vomit up water. I gasp for air, finally feeling it rush back into my lungs. As I look up, I see the singed stump of a tree, its broken body lying across the road, separating me from the monster. Celly flies above, and the sight of them fills me with gratitude.

The monster leaps over the fallen tree, her hand becoming a hammer. Without thinking I activate the wing spell I found in Seath's grimoire.

Massive, ethereal monarch butterfly wings appear on my back and carry me into the air and out of the path of the hammer.

Celly blasts her with lightning but it does very little, and in return she blasts them with a bolt of her own, knocking them to the ground.

"Celly!" I yell, that familiar rage building up inside me.

"Have you told that boy Kiran you have a crush on him yet?" the monster calls. "It would be such a shame if he were to drown tonight without ever knowing how you feel!"

"What?"

That moment of distraction is all it takes for her to shoot a lightning bolt at me. I have no time to dodge. I fall back to the earth, writhing as every muscle in my body tightens and spasms out of my control.

When I look up she is standing over me, her hand transformed into a spear. "Not that it matters. He likes Cara better than you."

I roll away from the monster and use my sigil to release a condensed blast of wind that tears her body apart, but the water just reforms into her shape with ease.

"Why wouldn't he?" she says, unphased. "Cara's obviously better than you in every way."

"Shut up!" I shout and release a shadow giant to attack her.

She avoids the giant's swinging arms and destroys it with a fireball. "She's prettier than you."

I fly up out of her reach as she runs at me with a spear hand again, but she turns her arm into a flurry of tentacles that reach up and clasp themselves around my legs.

"She's a better student than you!" she gloats as she uses the tentacles to slam me back into the ground, winding me.

"Even Seath thinks she would have been the better heiress to Yukiko," she says, walking over to me and stomping down on my chest. The air flies from my lungs.

I try to move her foot but I can't grip the water. I look up at that horrific, twisted smile, and see her arm transform into a spear again.

As she rears her arm back my mind goes blank, and all I can do is whisper, "Please don't."

Suddenly, a loud screech fills the air, making the monster clutch her ears and wail in pain. She lets out a vicious snarl and extends her arm to grab Celly, blocking their speakers with her fingers.

I look around for inspiration as I crawl away from the monster through the snow . . .

That's it.

I raise my sigil hand and focus as hard as I can as she throws Celly far away and begins menacing toward me again. Her steps abruptly become loud and heavy, and she starts to slow as all the water making up her body freezes. Before she can reach me, I completely solidify her.

I close my fist, and tendrils of shadow appear around her and crush her into a thousand shards.

As she is destroyed, I hear the disembodied giggle once again, and her fading voice echoes in the empty air. *"Seath Faolan is a murderer."*

I sit up in the snow, breathing heavily as the presence of magic disappears completely. What in the world was that horrible thing?

Celly comes flying back to me. "Are you okay, Selena?"

I nod. "My throat is burning and my back really hurts, but I'm okay. Can you get through to Seath yet? I don't think I can get up."

I can hear the phone ring in reply, and I crawl to the boulevard and lie back down, waiting for help.

X.

Jealousy

As I stand atop the clock tower balcony, I can't help but notice the clock is now firmly fixed at eleven o'clock. The time went down. I search the ocean in the sky above for the beast, and the surface begins to ripple.

I can sense something calling to the depths above, and I trace its source to the figure atop the school. I remember seeing—or perhaps hallucinating—the stranger's silhouette when the water apparition attacked me.

Their magical presence is the same. So my dream is trying to tell me they're connected? There has to be something more to this.

The great beast emerges from the ocean with a great crash, responding to the call.

On a building between myself and the stranger I can see another figure. I squint, something cold settling in the pit of my stomach as I recognize Kiran, sword in hand.

Suddenly he starts falling upwards, as if someone has flipped gravity in reverse.

"Kiran!" I call, to no avail.

He hits the sky-sea and pops back up, struggling to stay afloat amidst the tumultuous waves, but watery tentacles rise from the surface and ensnare him, dragging him to the depths.

When I wake up, I'm back in my room at Yukiko's house. My eyes hurt and my cheeks are wet from tears. I sit up, sniffling.

I can sense someone looking at me, and I realize the room is quite full as I open my eyes—my parents, Kiran, Cara, Seath, and Celly all crowd around on various chairs brought from downstairs.

"Selena!" Cara cries, jerking up and alerting everyone else as she leaps to my bedside and hugs me.

"Are you hurt?" Dad asks.

Mom rubs my back from the other side of the bed. "How are you feeling?"

"Don't crowd her!" Seath says fruitlessly—perhaps hypocritically, too, as he towers over the bed with a worried expression.

"I'm okay," I tell them, my voice still slightly hoarse.

I can see Kiran at the foot of the bed breathing a sigh of relief. He's gripping the poster of the bed so tightly that his knuckles have gone white.

"Tell us what happened," Seath says, drawing my attention away. "Celly says you were attacked by a water thrall."

"I sensed magic but it felt completely different from Yukiko and Cyra. It was like a whole new force I'd never experienced before. It was deep and terrifying," I start. "The monster . . . she looked just like me."

"The attacker fought viciously," Celly filled in. "We are lucky to have survived."

"Did she say anything?" Seath asks.

"She—" I look back at Kiran, and my voice trails off.

Have you told that boy Kiran you have a crush on him yet?

I can feel my cheeks getting warmer, but that's ridiculous. I don't have a crush on him. I guess he is really nice. He's brave, and cute, too. But I don't like him in that way. He's my friend.

"Selena? What did the monster say?"

"Nothing," I lie. Celly makes a face at me like they are disappointed, but they don't speak up.

After a while, everyone clears out to give me some space. As they leave, I call out, "Seath."

He lags behind, closing the door once only he and Celly are left. He leans against the door, his arms crossed, and looks at me expectantly. A lingering anxiety grips me, sitting heavy in my chest. I take a moment to collect my thoughts. I should tell him everything.

"I wasn't being honest before," I admit. "I didn't want Cara or Kiran to hear what the monster really said."

Seath nods meaningfully, and gestures for me to continue.

"She said Cyra was angry . . . what did she call her, Celly? It was weird."

"Big sister Cyra," Celly answers.

Seath scratches his chin through his beard and looks up at the ceiling as if seeing through it. "Continue."

"She taunted me. She said . . ." My voice trails off. It's a little embarrassing to admit, for some reason. "She told me that I have a crush . . . on Kiran. She said I should admit it before she gets the chance to kill him."

"Drown him," Celly corrects. "The thrall specifically threatened to drown him."

"She kept telling me how Cara was better than me, everyone likes her more than me, stuff like that . . ." I shake my head. "It was crazy."

"And is that how you feel?" Seath asks. "Are you jealous of her?"

I frown. That's ridiculous. Of course I'm not jealous of her. She's my best friend, I've known her all my life and I love her.

She's prettier than you.

I suppose that's true, she always looks great, and when she tries she can be really glamorous. On new years she was absolutely stunning. I guess in comparison I did look rather plain. But that doesn't really matter . . . does it?

She's a better student than you!

I guess she has always gotten better grades, even though sometimes I feel like I spend way more time on studying.

Even Seath thinks she would have been the better heiress to Yukiko!

Cara's already so talented as a spellcaster, and she's good at so many other things, too. Maybe if she was the Witch of the Half-Moon instead, she could have protected everyone better against Cyra. Maybe Seath wouldn't have lost his powers.

"Miss Selena? I asked you a question."

"I don't mean to be," I say, guiltily looking away from him.

"But you are jealous. Have you ever told anyone you feel this way? Like Kiran, your mom, even Celly?" he asks.

"Never!" I spit out, turning to him.

"Someone has been reading your thoughts," he mutters. "That's powerful magic. Reading the mind is extremely challenging because your thoughts are almost never coherent, from an outsider's perspective. It's like an ocean of abstract information, a puzzle that needs to be carefully assembled in a maze of puzzles. Who among Cyra's coven was skilled at such things?"

"Coven?" I remember Seath using that word before once, and both he and Kiran have said Cyra works with other witches.

"A coven is a group of witches who have formed a magical contract to unite their powers. Cyra's is the Golden Coven, and there are five witches involved. Not counting Cyra, there's the Witch of the Mountains, but this isn't her style. There's the Witch of Seasons, but if this was her doing we'd have seen her vassals Hazel and Florence by now. There's the Witch of the Unseen, but as far as I know she's in no condition to do something like this." He pauses, confusion crumbling his face. He opens up to speak twice in a row, but stops himself. "That's strange, I'm drawing a blank on the last member of the coven. I guess it has been over thirty years since I've seen any of them, though."

"Kiran probably knows," I say.

Seath nods. "In the meantime, I'll find some books for you on how to resist mind reading. Did the monster say anything else?"

Seath Faolan is a murderer.

"No," I say after a long pause. "Nothing."

I don't know why I didn't tell him. I just keep thinking back to when he met Kiran and immediately threatened him. Would he really have hurt Kiran then if Cara and I didn't stop him? What if what that creature said is true? Would I even really want to know? When I first met Seath I got this sense deep in my heart that he was safe, and I could trust him. But now my senses don't tell me anything about him.

The attack only seems to have made everyone more on edge. I thought that living with Cara and Kiran would be fun, but most of the time they are both off on their own, practicing and training. Even when I text Mom, all she ever seems to be doing these days is reading the books Seath gives her.

As I walk through the snow-covered garden behind the house, I can't recall ever feeling so lonely before in all my life. Is this really what I wanted? Maybe it would have been better to give up being Selena the Witch, and become Lyra the Normal Girl.

I decide to leave for school before the others. I know they'll be upset—everyone made a big deal about me never leaving the grounds alone because I might be attacked again, but if I were to be attacked I wouldn't want them around, anyways. If I have to choose between putting my friends in danger or facing this unknown enemy alone, I'd choose to go it alone every single time.

I arrive just as the school's custodian opens the front gates. I'm one of only a handful of students here at this hour, and perhaps the only one who isn't on one of the school's many sports teams. I drop my things off at my locker, including the package I intend to give Cara for her birthday today, and wander.

I find myself walking out to the athletics field. The hole I punched through the wall escaping Cyra is still there. I stare at it for a moment, lost in thought, before I dust the snow off of part of the bleachers and sit.

I suppose this is where it began for me—this is where I was summoned to Yukiko's house by that vision in September. I look up, almost expecting to see the moon, but there's nothing but clouds.

Celly buzzes, and I take them out. One—no, two missed texts from Cara.

Celly's avatar appears. "Shouldn't we answer her, Selena?"

They display the messages for me. 'Selena, where are you?' followed by 'Kiran can't find you, are you okay?'

So they're together right now.

He likes Cara better than you!

I shake my head and scowl. "Just tell them I'm at school."

"Is something wrong, dear?" a sweet voice calls.

I look over my shoulder to see Ms. Rivers alarmingly close. Did she see Celly? Did she catch me talking to them? How did I not hear her approaching? I quickly stuff them back in my pocket.

"Good morning, Ms. Rivers," I say with a feigned smile.

She clears off her own spot on the bleachers and sits beside me, her hands in her lap. "You don't have to fake being happy with me, Selena. Is everything okay?"

I nod. "I had kind of a hard weekend, but I promise I'm fine."

"Well, if you ever want to talk, you can always come see me. You know where the teacher's lounge is, I assume?"

I smile for real this time. "I know where to find it."

My eyes drift to her ring. I didn't get a good look at it last time, but it's really pretty. The silver ring features a teardrop-shaped diamond, with sea-green stones set in the band. Ms. Rivers catches me looking at it, and holds her hand up.

"My partner Alton gave it to me when he proposed," she says with a sad little smile. She stands up, brushing some lingering snow from her pants. "Shall we go?"

Ms. Rivers escorts me back to the school building. It made me feel a lot better, talking to her, even though I can't really tell her anything. I feel lucky that I ended up with her as my teacher. I guess I don't always appreciate enough how many kind people I'm surrounded by.

I head back to my locker to find Cara and Kiran waiting, both looking distressed. They notice me as I approach, and they both run over, with Cara hugging me.

"Why did you leave without us?" Cara demands, gripping my shoulders. "We promised we wouldn't go off alone anymore!"

Kiran's brow is furrowed as he glares at me. "What if something happened again?"

I show a weak smile and walk past them to my locker, taking out the package. "I'm sorry, I just didn't want you to see this before I gave it to you."

Cara takes it, inspecting it for a moment.

"Happy birthday!" I say meekly. "I'm sorry it's not as exciting as the bracers, but I thought you'd like it."

She unwraps it, revealing three mangas of the same series.

"You know, there's not really anything to do at Yukiko's, so I figured . . ." I say, gesturing to them. "Now you have something to read besides old books."

She smiles, and Kiran's expression softens, too. She looks at me as if she is going to say something else, but instead she just says, "Thank you."

There is an awkward tension in the air. There is a distance between us that I've never felt before. As we stand there looking at each other, it feels like we've left far too much unsaid between us.

XI.

The Pool

The weather has gotten quite frosty lately. Even as Kiran, Cara, and I huddle together on the school bus for warmth, the sounds of the aggressive winds are almost deafening. Ms. Rivers has to shout to be heard over it.

"Listen up everyone!" she calls, and the rowdy class quiets down. "As you know, today's field trip is all about teaching you important life skills. We're going to start with the swimming class, so for those of you who already know how to swim, you get a free morning to play around in the pool."

The class erupts into cheerful shouts, and Ms. Rivers has to yell over them. "After swimming lessons, we're going to have lunch, then we'll be doing a first aid and CPR course. Please don't wander. Stay where the teachers and chaperones can see you, and let's all have fun today!"

I wonder if we'll be practicing CPR on those silly-looking dummies you see in movies and shows. Come to think of it— "Cara, don't you already know CPR?"

"No, I know basic first aid, though. You have to learn it at the archery club to be a member," she replies.

The bus climbs a large hill, at the top of which is the cross-shaped community center building. As we reach the entrance, I look out the window and I can see the clock tower from my dreams only a few blocks away. Somehow, the sight of it gives me a sense of anxiety.

Even as we exit the bus and I make my way into the building I can't shake the feeling.

The temperature difference between indoors and outdoors is dramatic—the community center staff evidently have the heat cranked way up. It's almost uncomfortably warm, especially in my winter coat.

At Ms. Rivers' direction, the class congregates toward the back of the building, where the change rooms and lockers are. Part of me wants to keep Celly close, but phones aren't allowed in the pool area. With few other options, I change into my purple one-piece and place them in the locker with my other personal effects.

I can hear some of the other girls in class lamenting the dress code, which all but mandates one-pieces, but part of me is a little glad. I would be way too embarrassed to wear a bikini around Kiran—and if I was the only one *not* wearing one, I'd feel like a kid. Besides, the boys have to cover up, too.

Why am I even thinking about this? I shake the thoughts out of my head and wander out to the pool area. There are actually four pools—an Olympic-sized swimming pool for competitions and training, a wading pool for little kids, a deep pool with diving boards, and finally an absurdly large recreational pool. On weekends, this place is packed to the rafters, but it's a ghost town in the middle of the week at ten in the morning. Aside from a couple of elderly women in the big pool doing exercises, it's just our class.

Ms. Rivers takes just over half the class to the big pool where the swim instructor is waiting. The rest of us are left to our own devices.

Cara is a little unsteady on her feet without her glasses, so she stumbles her way over to me in her lime-green swimsuit with its adorable mini tutu around the waist. I smile at her for a moment—

She's prettier than you.

I look away and try to push the thought out of my head. That was just some crazy stuff the monster was saying to try and distract me, I'm not really jealous of her. I have to stop dwelling on that.

"Selena!" she says, catching my attention. "I really need prescription goggles, this is awful. I'm already getting a headache."

"Where's Kiran?"

Cara points to the tallest diving board. "That's him up there, isn't it?"

Sure enough, there he stands in his black trunks and steel grey sleeveless swim shirt. He stretches his back out, then walks to the edge of the diving board. He takes a deep breath, exhales, then leaps into the water. Cara and I clap for him as he swims over to the edge of the pool.

"Getting in?" he says, splashing us.

"Not like that I'm not," Cara retorts.

Two of the other boys in class challenge Kiran to a race in the Olympic pool, so he pulls himself out of the water. For a moment, as he climbs out every muscle in his arms are flexed, and as I watch, my brain tunes out everything else—I can't hear or see anything.

"Selena?"

Cara's voice catches me off guard and I stammer out, "W-what?"

"I asked if you wanted to watch them race!" she says with a smile.

I nod in agreement, but as I follow her and the boys to the other pool, I get an uncomfortable shiver down my spine, and I can sense something unpleasant. As Kiran and the other boys swim laps, Cara sits out of the way with her feet dipping in the water. I go to join her, but the closer I get the more uncomfortable I feel. My heart starts beating faster as I stand at the edge, and I feel this sickening aversion to the water.

"Cara, get out of the water," I say as the realization dawns on me.

"What's wrong?" she asks obliviously.

I grab her arm and start pulling. "Get out of the water!"

As she climbs to her feet I call out, "Kiran! Get out of the pool!" but he can't hear me over the splashing. One by one, as the boys cross the middle of the pool once again, they seem to become tangled in some invisible force. All three of them look around, confused.

"Kiran!" I yell again, catching his attention. "Come here!"

He tries to swim toward me but he can't. No matter how hard he kicks he's frozen in place.

Then they're all dragged underwater.

They fight to keep their heads above the surface, drawing the attention of the rest of the class.

"I'm going in," Cara says, readying herself to jump, but I hold her back.

"If you do, it'll get you too!"

"What is it?" she asks.

I shake my head. "I don't know!"

The swim instructor thoughtlessly dives in to grab the boys, but whatever is inside the water grabs him, too.

I need to do something, and fast. If I don't hurry—

Kiran and the others are dragged to the bottom of the pool. I can see them all struggling, fighting to get free, but they're completely stuck.

"Selena, he's going to drown! What do we do?" Cara cries.

It's just like my dream. He's been dragged below the water right before my eyes and I'm helpless . . .

No, I can't afford to be helpless. I'm tired of my friends getting hurt. I won't let Cyra or her allies take Kiran.

I need to see what I'm dealing with. I hold my sigil hand behind my back so no one can see the glow and generate a handful of black liquid that pours onto the floor and drains into the pool. The liquid clings to the invisible tendrils of the monster, revealing the vague shape of a woman's upper body and a squid-like lower body. Before anyone can notice, I call all the incredible force of the windstorm outside.

All the walls of the swimming area are glass—the wind shatters them and blasts the pool, freeing everyone and carrying the monster out as a formless mass of water.

I nod to Cara, who jumps in the pool as I run back to the locker room to grab Celly and summon my witch outfit. I throw it on over my swimsuit and run back into the main hall and to a fire exit near where I flung the monster.

As I burst through the door, setting off the fire alarm, I find the wind storm has gotten stronger and is now kicking up the snow. I can barely see anything through it, but I can feel that same strange presence. I let my senses guide my steps through the blizzard. The visibility is so poor I almost walk right into her, stopping myself in the shadow of her large frame.

"You spoiled my fun, brat!" she hisses.

Now that I can get a good look at the water monster, I can see that she is modeled after Cara—except that her face is upside down.

"I know your weakness now!" I shout.

I try to freeze the monster, but her body starts to thrash around and break down and reform to keep the water in motion, making it impossible to freeze her this way. Her tentacles lunge at me, but I cast the wing spell and launch myself high in the air.

"What do we do?" Celly calls.

If I can't freeze her, then maybe I can do something else. I summon the stars to send a hail of ice beams down from the sky, and just as I predicted, she warps her body to avoid being frozen. At the same time, I summon a shadow bubble to cover my sigil arm and I clench my fist.

"You hurt my friend," I spit out.

I rotate in the air and kick off of a magical burst of air to divebomb the monster. The surface of the water resists me and it feels like punching cement, but I break through, sinking my arm to the elbow in her belly. Her whole body returns to its original shape, and her twisted face looks down on me with rage.

I cast the flame circle from my grimoire into my hand and pour all of my energy into the flame. The water cannot penetrate the shadow bubble, but the more energy I pour into the flame, the hotter it gets. She coils her tendrils around me but her whole body starts to shudder as the water inside superheats and instantly begins boiling. She glares at me and I can see the realization growing in her eyes.

Her entire body explodes, the shockwave flinging me back.

"Selena," Celly calls. "You did it!"

I barely hear them. I barely do anything as I rush back inside the building, the only thing on my mind spilling from my lips as I run. "Kiran."

As I duck inside the changing room, Celly recalls my witch outfit and grimoire, and both are absorbed by them. I don't even pause. I just burst back into the pool room, coming to a halt when I see Kiran and the others who were attacked sitting on the bench, wrapped in towels, surrounded by the class.

As I walk over to them, Ms. Rivers blocks my path. "Where did you run off to?"

"To call for help," I lie, holding Celly up in their cell phone mode.

She nods, though she looks skeptical. "You're not the only one. A few others called nine-one-one. But I don't like that you left without telling me. I'm responsible for you, and if anything happened while you were out of my sight, it would have been my fault for not keeping better track of you."

"I'm sorry," I mutter.

She smiles gracefully. "I know you were worried about your friend. Go check on him, I'm sure he could use your care right about now."

I give her a smile in return, then run to Kiran. He stands as I approach, and I can't get any words out, so I just throw myself at him and hug him.

"Thank you," he whispers in my ear through his hoarse voice. "For saving me."

XII.

Sink into the Depths

The snow has piled up quite dramatically over the past few days. It's now knee-deep, and the school is closed today because of it. I bundle up and head out, Sovanna following me into the frigid outdoors. I use the flame spell to clear the pathways around the manor, the gardens, and the driveway so that Seath doesn't have to shovel it. The dog gleefully plays in the snow, jumping around and running up and down the driveway.

At least someone's happy.

As Sovanna starts to settle down, I walk over to pet her, but as I reach out and let her sniff my hand, she suddenly grows defensive. She backs away as if she's scared, her tail tucked and her fangs bared.

"Sovanna, what's wrong? It's only me," I say as I calmly take a step forward, but she starts growling and barking at me.

I back off, and she whimpers and runs off toward the house. I let her in from afar with magic, and then I am left alone in the cold.

With a heavy sigh, I walk around the house to stand by the lake. The water's surface has frozen over, though I'm not sure if it is solid enough to walk on.

There is something strangely enthralling about the frozen lake. It feels serene and peaceful. The snow across the surface seems to shimmer in the light, and it seems so inviting. I can almost feel something out there, drawing me in, like a friend leading me by the hand. My eyes are fixated on the distant shore, dusted with pretty snow.

I can hear a crack beneath my feet, and for a moment I'm distracted. I look at my feet and realize I'm on the ice. I freeze, waiting to see if the ice will give, but nothing happens. I shoot a glance back toward the manor, and a fuzzy feeling forms in my head, as if something inside is shouting at me but the voice is muffled and I can't understand it. Maybe I should go back . . . but I can't resist the call from the other side. Even just looking in that direction settles my nerves, and puts my mind at ease.

Maybe, if I cross the lake, I won't feel so alone anymore. There won't be any more fighting or fear. Just peace.

I see a figure in the trees on the other side. I can't make them out, but they are undoubtedly my friend. That fuzzy feeling in my skull comes back sharper than before, but every step that brings me closer to them makes me feel calmer.

"Selena!"

The scream echoes across the lake. I stop, finding myself at its center. I look back and see Seath shouting for me with Celly at his side, and a sense of anxiety starts to set in. There's a strange look on his face and it takes me a moment to register what it is—terror. What could they have to be afraid of? The sense of calm, the allure drawing me across the lake starts to fade like the breaking of a fog inside my mind, and my heart begins to race. What am I doing out here?

"Come back!" he shouts.

I look back at the other side of the lake, and the figure is gone. I take a step towards Seath, but the ice gives off a sickening crack.

"The ice!" I shout back, my heart thundering in my chest. "It's breaking!"

Cara and Kiran come running, but Seath drops his cane, grabbing their arms and pulling them back from the ice. Kiran tries to pull himself free, but even from afar I can tell Seath's grip is like an iron vice.

"Use your magic and freeze it!" Seath commands.

As I reach my hand out and my sigil starts to glow, a woman's voice echoes in my head and gives me pause. *Sink into the depths.*

As if responding to her words, the ice below me shatters.

The water is so cold I can't think. I flail helplessly toward the surface, but some invisible force keeps dragging me down. Every attempt I make to breathe just fills my lungs with water. I choke and gag, and the cold feels like a thousand needles stabbing me both inside and out.

A figure stands upright at the bottom of the lake. It stings to keep my eyes open, but I can't look away. The dark keeps her face obscured, but I can just vaguely make out a sea-blue robe and witch hat, and on her chest is a sigil unlike any I've seen. The centerpiece represents the sea, and there are seven symbols surrounding it inside the circle.

As I stare at her, my urge to fight weakens, and I allow myself to drift closer to the bottom. My vision starts to fade, and it feels as if I'm falling asleep.

The last thing I hear is a crashing sound from above. As my eyes seal shut a warm arm wraps around me and drags me away from the woman.

I am back in the dream, and just like before, the great sea serpent crashes through the ocean in the sky, flying over the school.

When I look back, the clock tower is frozen at ten o'clock.

I look out toward the school. Sure enough, just as I thought, the figure in the distance wears the same sea-blue robes as the woman I saw beneath the ice. She's a witch, like me.

Something compels me to look down into the plaza below. My heart drops to my feet as I see Cara, Kiran, and Seath unconscious.

"It's your fault," the woman's voice whispers in my ear. "They are going to die because of you."

"No!" I scream, and my eyes pop open.

I gasp for air and begin coughing, nausea crawling up my throat.

I look around, though my vision is foggy and my eyes hurt. It takes a moment for my eyes to adjust. I'm in the house, in front of the fire, with Cara huddled up next to me, and I'm wrapped up in several layers of blankets and towels. Kiran sits beside us, holding me up.

"C-cold," I stutter through chattering teeth. Seath kneels in front of me and offers me a large mug full of hot tea.

"Drink it slow and steady. We have to bring your body temperature back up carefully," he says.

The tea tastes strongly of lemon, and each sip is so warm and comforting. Celly flies up in front of me, looking me over. It almost looks like they have tears in their eyes.

"What happened?" Celly asks.

"I-I went out by the lake to think, and–and it was like I couldn't control m-myself. I saw a-a figure on the other side, and I just had this . . . uncontrollable urge to follow them, s-s-so that's what I did," I explain. "The last thing I remember is th-the ice breaking, and seeing a w-woman down there, at the bottom of the lake. A witch. She was casting some kind of spell, and then that was it, I passed out."

"You almost drowned, but Cara and Kiran saved you. Cara stabilized the ice with her magic, and Kiran dove into the breach after you," Seath explains.

"I thought this house was safe," Celly says. "You said there were magical protections in place."

Seath groans as he struggles to get up, collapsing on the couch. "It is safe. The wards and spells Yukiko wove into the grounds and the very walls of the house itself are designed to repel magical attacks, block curses, block foresight and even foretelling magic, and of course block unfriendly witches. Cyra may be the most powerful woman alive right now, and not even she could set foot here. Kiran was only allowed to enter because Selena invited him. But these protections only extend to the house and the grounds."

"So that woman was luring Selena away from the house so she could hurt her?" Celly asks.

"I'm afraid so. It seems Selena's been bewitched to respond to the woman's call. She probably got to you while you were distracted fighting that monster at the pool, or before with the thrall in the streets," Seath says. "I'm sorry, if I still had my powers, I would have been able to sense this."

"It was just like when I first came here," I say, staring into the fire. "It felt just the same as that vision."

I try to recall the look of that strange sigil—perhaps Seath would recognize it—but when I think back to it, my memory of it is all fuzzy, as if the details have been blocked by a fog in my mind.

From the corner of my eye, I can see Kiran scowling. "Enough is enough. This whole time I've been completely useless because I don't have my powers. Selena, I need you to make me your vassal. I can't sit on the sidelines anymore."

XIII.

Hostile

The half-moon sits high above us all as we gather around my sigil formed in ice on the floor of the garden.

I stand just outside of the circle as Kiran kneels in the center, and Seath, Cara, and Celly watch. I activate the sigil on the ground and it begins to glow. Kiran bows his head and offers his scarred hand to me, and just as Seath instructed me, I step into the circle and take his hand into both of mine, making sure my sigil hand is on top.

"Kiran Hoku, I call upon you to bear the power of the Half-Moon and serve as my emissary and vassal," I recite the phrase just how I was told to.

"I pledge myself in service to the Witch of the Half-Moon. I shall take on your burdens and rise as your subject," he replies.

The sigil on my hand lights up in response. I am meant to transfer some of my power to him, to give him the ability to use my magic. But for some reason, my heart's not in it. Is this really what I want? Or am I just sharing my magic with him because he told me to? Magic is supposed to be about imagination and willpower, but where is my will in all of this? I got my powers because Yukiko wanted me to have them. I fought against Cyra because Yukiko planned for me to. And I'm giving my powers to Kiran now because that's what he said I should do.

Perhaps I'm overthinking it. I try to focus on imprinting my powers onto him, but eventually the light of the sigils fades away, and as I move my hands I can see that nothing has happened.

Kiran pounds the ground with his fist. "Dammit! Try again!"

"We've tried four times already," Seath says. "She needs to rest."

He scoffs in reply and storms away. I want to sympathize, but his attitude just frustrates me for some reason. I just feel like grabbing him and yelling at him to stop putting all this pressure on me.

As if sensing my thoughts, Seath puts his hand on my shoulder. "It's hard, losing your powers. He must be incredibly frustrated seeing you be attacked time and time again while he can't help. He's a good young man, and for someone like Kiran, it goes against every instinct in his body to not throw himself between you and danger."

"As if I'd want him to do that?" I snap, shuffling out of Seath's reach. "I didn't take his powers away, Cyra did that!"

He doesn't answer. We share a look as my brow furrows, but after a few seconds my expression softens, and I'm overwhelmed with guilt. That wasn't like me.

I wonder if I should apologize, but he just wanders away without saying anything. I look at Cara, but she shakes her head at me.

"We've all made sacrifices for you, you know," she mutters.

"I never asked you to sacrifice anything," I reply.

She glares at me. "What did you expect us to do when you were in danger? Just stand by and watch? We jumped in because that's what friends do, but none of us signed up for this."

"I appreciate that, but why are you mad at me?" I fire back. I can feel my face getting hot with rage. It's not fair to blame everything on me.

"Because you're not thinking about us!" Cara explodes. "You just expect us to go along for the ride, but I had my own life before Cyra came and it didn't revolve around you! Kiran and I gave up everything for you, and you have never returned the favor," she shouts.

My hands ball into fists. "Tell me, then, what should I have done instead? Not fight back?"

"That's exactly what you should have done!" Cara yells. "You should have let Cyra take your powers away. If you did that, none of this would be happening."

Tears of frustration fill my eyes. "Is that what you really think?"

"I miss my family!" Cara cries, tears now falling down her cheeks. "I want to go home! I hate this house!" She shakes her head. "I hate all of this!"

"Go, then!" I shout back. "I've fended off both attacks without your help, I don't need you!"

The minute the words leave my lips I regret saying them.

Cara flinches as if she'd been struck. I can't begin to understand what's wrong with me, this isn't who I am.

"Cara–" I begin, but she runs off.

I wipe my eyes and try to suppress any more tears from falling.

She's probably right. Everything is my fault. I'm ruining their lives, both of them, by dragging them into my problems. Cara wouldn't have to be stuck here if it wasn't for me. She wouldn't have to be fighting. Kiran would still have his powers. I've made a mess of everything. I don't know what Yukiko saw to make her choose me as her heir, but she made a mistake.

Eventually, I walk back to the house to go looking for Kiran. I knock at his door, and after a moment with no answer I carefully open it, announcing, "I'm coming in."

He sits with his back to me, Sovanna's head in his lap as he pets her fur slowly. "What do you want?" he spits out.

I fiddle with my hands. "I got into a fight with Cara and–"

"She left?"

"Yeah," I mutter.

He turns to face me, a strange glare across his face. I've never seen him look so aggressive. "Without her, this is more important than ever," he says. "You need to take this seriously and give me some of your power."

I shake my head. "I *am* taking this seriously, and I *am* trying to!"

"You're not trying hard enough!" he bellows. "I lost my powers for you, and I was counting on you to restore them and you just keep letting me down!"

"Kiran," I stammer, stunned. "I–I–"

"You turned out to be a disappointment," he says with pure venom in his voice.

The tears I'd been holding back break through. I can't stop them anymore. I back away from him and run to my room. I throw my back against the door and wail into my hands. The tears stream out until my eyes sting and feel puffy, and my cries subside to sniffles. After a few minutes, I look around the room. I wipe my eyes and retrieve my backpack and a duffel bag and start packing them.

Celly flies from my pocket and observes me as I stuff my bag with different things, summoning my grimoire and witch outfit to pack.

"Are you leaving?" Celly asks. I nod. "Is that a good idea?"

"It doesn't matter. I just can't be here anymore," I say as I stuff my bags full and zip them both up.

Celly looks worried. They keep moving to stay in my line of sight. "Are you going home?"

"If I went home I'd just put Mom and Dad in danger, too," I reply.

"Then where are you going to go?" Celly asks.

I open the door and start making my way downstairs.

"Maybe you should think about this before you do anything rash," Celly says.

"I'm sorry," I whisper.

I turn on my heels and hold my sigil hand out to Celly. I draw from our connection to each other, and using my powers I force them to sleep. Celly's avatar disappears, and they fall to the floor, completely dormant. I pick them up and gently set them down on the living room table.

"I can't let you get hurt again, either," I say, hoping they can hear me in their slumber.

Everyone is disappointed in me, and I've hurt them all by making them a part of this. It's time I make things right. I might not be able to give Kiran or Seath their powers back, but I can make sure nobody else suffers for my sake. With that in mind, I leave the sanctuary of Yukiko's home and head out into the world.

At first I'm not sure where to go—the weather conditions are still quite treacherous, and I find myself walking aimlessly. But the more I think, the more I feel like it doesn't matter, as long as where I go is far away from here. I take cover behind a tree for a moment and cast the fairy wings spell, and I fly off over the woods, staying close to the treetops to avoid being seen.

XIV.

Isolation

I don't know how long I've been flying for. It feels like it's been days, but the sun is only starting to set. There is something in the air that keeps me moving, no matter how tired I feel. Some menacing feeling that assails my senses. Every part of my soul is screaming *'danger!'*, and if I so much as slow down, the anxiety grows so intense that I can hardly breathe.

I keep to the trees as much as possible, flying low and moving in a single direction. I only shift directions to cross the occasional road or highway.

I keep going as far as my wings will take me, but I still can't shake the relentless, oppressive fear that something is waiting around every corner and behind every tree, ready to take me the second I land.

As the dawn begins to break I find myself slowing, my body beginning to protest my will to keep running. The bags have begun to feel like impossibly heavy weights, and my flying is starting to grow clumsy. As I approach a creek cutting through the wilderness, my wings start to give out. I drop from the sky at an alarming pace and cast several consecutive barriers of air to slow my crash into the snow.

Though I'm not really hurt, the crash leaves me sobbing in frustration. I drag myself to my knees and crawl over to a tree with no snow underneath. I sit with my back against it and hug my knees to my chest, shivering. It's so cold out here.

Why is all of this happening? Just because Cyra had some grudge against Yukiko, I end up out here, alone. I wish Yukiko had told me the reason. There's so much I don't know, so many secrets. I look down at Yukiko's ring on my finger. Despite its lunar imagery, it doesn't feel like the powers of the moon were used to create or even enchant it. The more I try to connect with it, the more it feels like–

She said it was a gift, though she never told me who it was from.

I let out a sigh. I should have realized sooner. Cyra Oralie created this ring. Cara once said it looked like an engagement ring. I wonder if Seath really didn't know, or if he was just trying to hide the truth.

Wiping my eyes, I pull myself to my feet and shuffle over to the duffle bag I dropped and retrieve it. Looking around, I can see a town in the distance. The mere sight of civilization reminds me that I haven't eaten in almost twenty-four hours, I'm cold, and I desperately want a shower. I guess I can't exactly get a hotel room since I don't have a credit card. I don't have much in the way of money in general, maybe a hundred dollars or so in cash? At the very least, I could get something to eat. I can figure out where to sleep after.

I drag my feet along, following the creek down the valley toward town. Partway through the trek, though, I sense something strange. Something is calling me in the other direction, away from the creek. The allure is soothing and warm. Each step I take toward the source of the mysterious siren seems to alleviate my sore ankles, rumbling stomach, and tiredness.

I wander into a large, muddy clearing, and on the other side is the woman from under the lake. She stands in the shadow of a tree, her hat obscuring her face. She keeps a sword on her hip, and I can sense incredible magical energy emanating from it. The top buttons of her renaissance blouse are open, revealing the sigil on her chest.

Wait a moment. She's dangerous, isn't she? Why am I walking toward her? She's the one who tried to drown Kiran and I, who sent monsters after me. Why is it that I feel so calm?

The thoughts disappear like smoke in the air. It doesn't matter, really. It's so peaceful.

It seems Selena's been bewitched to respond to the woman's call.

I stop dead in my tracks, halfway across the field. Something isn't right here. My sigil suddenly begins to glow, and the sense of calm and comfort throughout my body and mind immediately disappears. I stumble, the weight of my exhaustion, frustrations, fears, and everything else flooding back into my mind, and I look up at the strange woman.

"You've been controlling me?" I shout.

She raises both hands to her chest and invokes her sigil once more, and in response two water monsters come from the trees and take on their forms. One is made of boiling hot water. The left side of his body takes the form of a human, but the right is a coiling mass of small tendrils. The other is made of near-frozen ice water, and his body is a mirror image of his companion. But it's the faces that stand out most to me. The boiling face wears a grotesque grin, while the cold face is frozen in an anguished expression. I hardly recognize who it's meant to be until they stand side by side—it's Kiran's face.

"This could have been so easy for you," the monsters speak in unison. "You could have died peacefully, but now you have to suffer!"

The cold monster stretches his tendrils at me while the boiling one spews water toward me. I throw my bags down and dodge, using my sigil to tear my bag apart and bring my grimoire to my hand. I quickly summon my wings back and take to the sky, but both monsters sprout wings of their own and pursue me.

If the cold monster's body is already at freezing temperature, then the same trick I used on the last monster might work again.

Just like before, I coat my arm in a shadow bubble and fly at him, igniting a flame in my hand to superheat his body. The other monster spews another stream of water at me, but I summon an intense barrage of winds to throw the stream off course.

I twist my body to keep the cold monster below me so that when his body explodes it launches me further up in the air.

Now, suspended high in the sky, I call forth the stars, and at the same time I surround myself in a tumultuous storm of wind and divebomb the boiling monster. The wind shields me as I blast right through the monster, and then the stars bombard the fragments with freezing lasers, sending the chunks falling and shattering against the ground as I land.

My wings disappear on their own, and I fight every urge in my body to keep myself from passing out. It takes every ounce of strength to stay standing.

Before I can catch my breath, water droplets begin to levitate all around the field, and all at once they fly at each other, combining. The twin monsters reform, completely intact, and they laugh mockingly.

"You really think you can beat us with old tricks?" they say in tandem, their voice overlapping. "We were made to destroy you."

The boiling monster whips his tendrils forward, scalding my skin as it knocks me backwards. I struggle to climb to my feet, but I feel so weak and depleted, my magic a frail thread that I keep failing to grasp. The cold

134

monster drags me through the mud with his frosty hand, toward a puddle barely a foot deep. I struggle against him, but I can't seem to muster any power.

"Don't fight," they say. "Sleep."

As the cold monster holds my face over the puddle, I can hear a woman's voice whisper, "Seath took everything from me. Now, I'll take you from him."

Just then, I sense a burst of magic, and the cold monster releases me, his body half-frozen and bent awkwardly over the puddle. I crawl back from him to see the boiling monster explode from an arc of lightning.

I keep backing away as the cold monster sheds his frozen parts and pursues me, malformed, until Celly appears at my side and blasts him apart with wind.

"On your feet, Miss Selena," Seath's voice commands from my side. He extends his hand to me, saying, "This fight is far from over."

As the monsters reform, Cara stands armed to the south, and on the north side of the clearing is Kiran. Cara uses her grimoire to imbue Kiran's sword with both fire and lightning before readying an ice arrow for herself.

"You're all here! How?" I say through tears of relief.

"The second I got home after our fight I felt instantly better, and I realized what was happening," Cara explains.

"You were under that woman's spell," Kiran yells. "Every time we got close to you, it would trigger and embellish all of our negative emotions. She was trying to drive us apart!"

"Cara used her powers to wake me up, and I tracked you here," Celly adds.

"We won't ever abandon you, no matter how much she tries to mess with our minds!" Cara says, trying to fight off the boiling monster with her frost arrows.

Kiran keeps slashing the cold monster to bits, but no matter how many times he does, it reforms. "We won't give up!"

Seath unsheathes the blade hidden in his cane and holds it up in front of Celly. "Dazzle me, shortstop."

A whirlwind of air magic surrounds Seath's sword, and a wild look comes over him. He rushes in to fight alongside Cara, ferociously swinging his imbued blade at the monster. Celly joins Kiran, supporting him just in time to prevent him from being overwhelmed.

No matter how many times the water thralls are destroyed, they keep coming back. The first monster that attacked me would come back when her body was blown apart, but she was destroyed after I froze her. The second monster was destroyed, too, after I exploded her core. So, regardless of how resilient and fluid these monsters are, there must be some sort of nucleus controlling them, something that can be destroyed. I just have to find it.

Everyone is here to fight for me. They've given me this chance to find the source, so I can't let them down. I close my eyes and control my breathing. I inhale slowly and count down from three before exhaling. I tune out the sounds of the battle and give my consciousness entirely to my senses. I can feel the magic dancing in the air, the powers of the moon clashing against the mysterious aura of the water monsters. Yet the monsters are not the source of the aura. It's like the magic is being broadcast from somewhere else, and the monsters are just receivers for it.

Where is the source?

Why did the monster try to drown me in that small puddle instead of finishing me off where I was?

On instinct I walk to the puddle, and my hand grows snow white. I reach in and feel something, and as I do the form of a small fish turns to solid ice at my touch. I grasp it and pull it free from the puddle and open my eyes.

Both monsters abandon their battles and make a mad dash at me as I hold their conjoined heart in my hand. With my last ounce of strength I crush it, causing the monsters to turn into ordinary water and splash harmlessly against the earth.

Not a moment later, my body finally gives in to the exhaustion, and I drift into unconsciousness.

XV.
Tryouts

Six o'clock. The clock tower in the dream world has reached the halfway point. Just like always, the sea serpent breaks through the water above and hangs menacingly over the school.

"What are you trying to tell me?" I shout. "I know you're still out there!"

I wake before I get an answer. I huff at the ceiling, fighting the urge to scream into my pillow. How was Yukiko able to make sense of these dreams? What good is a prophetic dream if I can't figure out what it means? Seath said that there was no real trick to it, I'd just have to work it out for myself, which is frustrating and unhelpful advice.

I drag myself out of bed and stretch, then I grab an outfit and wander off to the shower to get ready for school.

I'm the first one down to the kitchen this morning. Judging from the creaking above, someone else is starting to get up. Slow, muffled, but sporadic footsteps, as if the person above me was dragging their feet or struggling to get them working first thing in the morning. A smile pulls at my cheeks. Definitely Cara.

I make her a coffee, and it's ready just a few moments before I hear her coming down the stairs. She drifts in with a grumpy expression, her glasses stuck and hanging in her messy hair.

"Good morning," I chirp with a bemused smile.

She groans in reply, and I helpfully point to her mug on the counter, which she retrieves and sips in misery, leaning against the counter and waiting for the rest of her brain to wake up.

I gently pull her glasses free from her hair as she ineffectually bats at my hand, and I set them down beside her.

"Hang in there," I say with an affectionate pat to her shoulder.

It's wonderful to see her back to her normal self.

I hear another set of steps upstairs—even, firm footsteps paired with the thunderous tip-tapping of blunt claws against the hardwood. That's Kiran and Sovanna for sure. I walk out to the foyer to meet them, and Sovanna charges down the stairs, tail wagging, to sniff and brush up against me affectionately.

"Sovanna, sit!" Kiran calls as he climbs down the stairs, smiling at me for a moment before his usual more stoic expression takes over.

He's smiling a lot more now that the spell has been broken, and it's quite charming.

"I was about to take Sovanna for a walk, do you want to come?" he says as he slips his shoes on.

"Yeah," I say, throwing mine on as well.

We walk around the house to the lake and saunter side by side as Sovanna runs off through the woods, exploring and sniffing at everything she can find. It's still chilly, but a lot of the snow has melted, and the lake is unfrozen. It feels like we're finally on the verge of spring.

"So. . ." he begins, his voice awkwardly trailing off.

I stifle a small laugh. Definitely back to normal. "You know, I was wondering something, about the spell we were under."

"What is it?" he asks.

I kick at a pebble with my toe. "Everyone, even Sovanna, was influenced by the spell, but it never seemed to affect Seath. I wonder why?"

Kiran thinks for a moment. "Strong-willed people can be very difficult to influence with magic. Cyra used to tell me that spells like that are especially cruel, because they draw out people's insecurities and doubts and weaknesses. So, if I had to guess, I would say that it didn't affect Seath because he didn't have any doubts the witch could exploit."

He looks away from me, as if ashamed. I'm not sure what I can tell him in this moment. The fact that the spell affected him doesn't make him seem weak—if anything, I think he's quite strong for overcoming it the way he did, and coming to rescue me with Cara. I wouldn't fault him for having doubts about me or his choice.

I glance at his scarred hand and tap it gently. "Does it hurt?"

He shakes his head. "No, it's just frustrating. If I had a sigil I could be doing so much more to help you."

I look away from him. "I'm sorry I couldn't make you my vassal."

He stops, grabbing my hand, and my heart feels like it has jumped up into my throat as my gaze swings to his.

"I need you to know," he says, looking intensely into my eyes. "I didn't mean what I said when I was under the influence of that spell. You are not a disappointment. I understand that sharing your power is incredibly difficult, especially after Cyra tried to steal it from you. I never should have pressured you."

"Kiran," I begin. His earnestness makes me feel a little embarrassed. What do I say? As the silence between us lingers, I grow more and more aware of just how close we actually are; our toes are almost touching, and the cool, minty scent on his breath fills my nostrils. I can feel myself getting warm in the face, and I'm suddenly hyper-aware of a million potential miniscule flaws with myself. Does my hair look okay? Isn't my outfit kind of drab? Do I look tired? Did I brush my teeth well enough? Did I remember to put on deodorant? I'd almost forgotten that he still has my hand tangled in his, and when he reminds me with a small, perhaps even unintentional squeeze, it sends a jolt like lightning right through to my chest.

His posture shifts, and he starts to slink away from me, and I instinctively squeeze his hand back.

"Umm!" *Say something!* "You . . . I'm glad you're here . . . with me."

The next second feels like an hour. All I can hear is my heart thumping, and I scrutinize his expression for even the most minor hint at what he might be thinking, until finally his lips curl into a crooked smile.

"I'm glad, too," he replies, putting my mind at ease. I let out a contented sigh. He's so comfortable to be around.

He interlocks his fingers with mine, and we ease back into our walk, hand in hand. I say nothing, I just walk in step with him, listening to the rhythm of his steps and his breathing.

When Sovanna returns to us finally, we part and walk back to the house to collect the now fully conscious Cara for school, leaving the dog in Seath's care.

School seems to breeze by, and the last bell quickly catches up to us. As it happens, Cara, Kiran and I all ended up in different classes for final period, so I wait for them by the school entrance for a couple of minutes before I realize they're not coming. I shake my head. Of course Cara has club activities, and baseball tryouts are today. Kiran is definitely there.

Come to think of it, there's no baseball field at school. Where would tryouts be?

"Waiting for someone?" The voice catches me off guard. For a minute it sends a sense of panic through my whole body, but when I turn to look, it's only Ms. Rivers.

"My friend is at baseball tryouts, I was thinking I'd go and watch," I explain.

She makes a sympathetic face. "They take a bus there, but I think they already left."

"Oh," I mutter, looking down at my feet. That's a shame, I would have liked to have cheered him on.

"It's only a fifteen-minute walk from the school, though," she says. "Why don't I escort you there?"

I nod and smile at her. I quickly text Cara where I'm headed, and I walk alongside Ms. Rivers. She is quiet for the first little bit of our walk, but eventually, she breaks the silence.

"That's a pretty cool tattoo on your hand there," she says. "Did your parents let you get it, or was this a little act of teenage rebellion?"

"I guess you could say my parents were okay with me getting it. Do you have any?" I ask, desperate to change the subject.

"Can you keep a secret?" she says playfully. "I've got one too, but it's not very professional so I keep it covered up at work."

"What's it of?"

"The sea," she says with a smile.

I wonder what it looks like. I don't know how a tattoo of the sea could come off as unprofessional, but maybe it's in a weird place.

We eventually find our way to the baseball field. I spot Kiran right away—he's showcasing his batting skills.

Ms. Rivers directs us to a nearby playground up a short hill, and she sits on one of the old swings, gesturing for me to sit with her. The swings are positioned perfectly for a good view of the whole field, so as I swing lazily, I watch Kiran as he bats.

There's something endearing about his serious expression, followed by the cocky smirk he flashes when he hits the ball far enough to send the outfielders running after it. In his baseball uniform he's quite handsome, though with the cool February breeze in the air I imagine he's probably freezing right now. He's still not used to the cold, after all.

"You're thinking about something good, aren't you?" Ms. Rivers says suddenly, drawing me from my thoughts.

"What do you mean?" I ask, looking at her with my head cocked to the side.

"You've been smiling to yourself the whole time, like you've got your own private little joke over there," she says. She follows my gaze, smiling slightly when she sees Kiran. "Kiran Hoku, from homeroom. That's who you're here to see, isn't it?"

I can feel my cheeks start to go red despite my effort to suppress it. "Yes," I squeak out meekly.

"And are you two–"

"No!" I blurt out, perhaps a bit too loudly and quickly.

Ms. Rivers laughs to herself as my embarrassment rises. "I'm sorry, I don't mean to presume," she says as her chuckles subside. "He cares about you. I hope you treasure the time you have together now, while you have the chance to."

There is something off about that last part. It almost feels as though it came from a completely different person than Ms. Rivers. I open my mouth to ask what she meant, but Kiran waves at me and I push it out of my mind, waving back.

Cara joins us just as tryouts are ending, so I say my goodbyes to Ms. Rivers, and the three of us walk home together.

That night, I find myself struggling to get to sleep. No matter how much I toss and turn, I can't seem to get comfy. I climb out of bed, exasperated, figuring maybe some water and a snack might help, but something catches my eye as I start toward the door.

I turn to the window and peer outside, just able to see up the driveway in the moonlight. In the distance, I can see Sovanna meandering around. I frown, searching around for Seath or Kiran.

I see Seath just a bit further up, talking to a strange figure. I wonder who it is, especially at this hour? Maybe he's sneaking late-night takeout? But neither of them are holding anything. When I blink the figure is gone, and Seath has begun returning to the house.

XVI.
Claws of the Wolf

It seems like we're drawing closer to the end. The clock shows five o'clock.

There is something strange about the dream this time. There is an unsettling sense of dread in the air, and it plays out differently from the previous iterations. The sea serpent hasn't shown up, and where the mysterious figure usually is, there are two people this time.

I look away from them and into the distance, trying to figure out what the dream is trying to tell me. Is this a warning, or guidance? The world is still, yet that only makes the sinking feeling in my chest grow stronger. Huffing, my gaze travels back to the two figures. Their postures have changed ever so slightly. I can't put my finger on exactly why it makes me so uncomfortable, but then I realize—they're facing me now.

I blink and the taller figure is suddenly inches from my face. I scream and fall back in surprise, my heart racing in my chest as I clumsily scoot away from the figure. Wildly, I raise my eyes, trying to figure out—Seath?

Seath's face stares back at me, water pouring from his eyes and mouth–not tears, but seawater–with the word *murderer* written on his forehead in blood.

He tears his shirt to reveal his torso is glass, and I can see through to his glass organs. It looks like a cartoon depiction of his anatomy, like one you might see in a textbook. But what catches my attention is that inside his stomach is a shrimp-like creature burrowing thin wires that coil around everything inside of him.

Seath leans in close, the seawater from his mouth drenching me as he says, "A man whose body is awake while his mind sleeps is lost in his dreams."

I wake up just as the sun is starting to peak over the horizon. Trying to blink away the dream, I walk to the window, only to see that Seath is still out there, alone, in the driveway. That's strange. He didn't stay out there all night, did he? I get up and throw my witch outfit on— we'll be training this morning, anyway.

Eventually, Celly and I are joined by Kiran and Cara, and the four of us head out to the lake to get started. I find a large rock that's relatively clean and dry to sit on with mine and Seath's grimoires, then watch Cara warm up with her bow while Kiran stretches.

Cara freezes and looks into the distance for a moment, then catches Kiran's attention and walks toward me.

"What's Seath doing over there?" she says quietly, pointing across the lake.

I squint, following her finger. I hadn't noticed him at all. He must have wandered around from the front of the house—but then why did he take such a roundabout route? Why not just come from the gardens and walk along the shore?

"Let's go see, maybe he has a training plan for us today," Celly says.

As we walk around the lake, I keep my eyes on him. There's something eerie about him. He's just standing there, perfectly still, staring at the lake. I don't know why, but he's making me incredibly uncomfortable. Perhaps this is an after-effect of the spell that almost drove us all apart?

But as we get closer, I start to realize what it is that makes me feel so uneasy. I can sense two presences from where he's standing. It's subtle, but it's as if something is hiding in his shadow. Something sinister.

I look back toward the house, and my eyes start to widen in horror. I quickly grab Cara and Kiran by the arm.

"Run back to the house!" I say.

Kiran gives me a quizzical expression, tilting his head. "What's wrong?"

From the corner of my eye I can see Seath move with blinding speed, and I yank Kiran toward me just in the nick of time as Seath releases and swings his cane-sword through the air where Kiran's neck would have been.

"Seath?" Cara yells, fumbling to draw her bow.

He swings at her, but she casts a magic barrier to block the blow. The spell absorbs the brunt of it, but he kicks her down and turns his attention to me.

"What's wrong with him?" Celly asks.

I get a sick feeling in my stomach. This is what my dream was trying to warn me about last night. "He's got to be possessed somehow!"

I turn and start to run, but he leaps over me, landing in my path. I can sense the magic inside him. Whatever is controlling him is using his body as a conduit to cast spells.

He stalks toward me, his expression vacant. His movements have a twisted jerkiness, as if he were a puppet.

Kiran rushes past me and tries to duel Seath sword-to-sword as Cara comes to my side.

"Is it another water monster?" she says, drawing her arrow. "They all kind of looked like us, right?"

"No!" I reply. "I can sense it, it's the real Seath. The monster is inside his body, controlling him, so whatever we do, we have to destroy it without hurting him."

"I'm more worried about him hurting us," Cara says.

She's got a point. Seath's ferocity is too much for Kiran, and after only a few moments, he parries one of Kiran's swings and snatches the sword right from his hand before kicking him away. He flings Kiran's sword into the lake and thrusts his own blade towards Kiran, but Celly quickly fires a wind blast knocking Kiran to safety.

"Friendly fire!" Cara shouts.

"I calculated that my attack may not be strong enough to stop Seath, but it was most definitely strong enough to launch Kiran out of the way. If we survive, I will apologize after," Celly says.

"Try freezing him!" I say as Seath stalks toward us.

Cara nods and fires an ice arrow toward his feet, but a jet of water shoots from the lake, destroying it. Before she can ready another he lunges, using the blade to knock her bow from her hands and picking her up off her feet by the throat.

I focus on freezing him just like the first water monster. He turns to me, dropping Cara and thrusting his sword toward my open hand. I quickly multicast both my wings and the physical enhancement spell, and I jump out of the way and take to the air where he can't reach me.

His skin starts to look sickly pale, and his movements are slowing.

"Seath's body temperature is getting dangerously low," Celly yells, flying over to me. "His heart will stop if this continues."

I immediately cut off the spell. This won't work. I won't be able to freeze the monster inside without putting his life in danger. If I remember right from my dream, the weird shrimp creature was in his stomach . . . so perhaps with a concentrated hit, I can hurt it without seriously injuring him.

I reorient my body in the air and cast minor air blasts at my feet to kick off from, and I fly right at him as fast as possible. I twist in the air and hit his sword hand with a burst of wind to keep him from skewering me, and I crash feet-first into his gut with all my might.

The kick winds him and pushes him back, but he remains on his feet. It seems the monster is strengthening his body as well to resist blunt strikes.

He tries to stab me, so I kick off him and try to fly away, but I feel his hand clamp down on my ankle. He swings me, turns on his heels, and slams my body into a nearby tree. I collapse to the ground, gasping from the pain. Everything is a blur, and my head feels as though it's been split in two.

As my vision comes into focus I see him towering over me, but something is wrong. His expression, ever so slightly, has shifted. He no longer has an empty stare, he almost looks . . . scared.

He grabs his head and looks away from me for a moment, stumbling and swaying violently as I crawl backward.

Kiran stumbles to my side and helps me to my feet. "What's wrong with him?"

Seath lets out a beastly howl and begins slamming his head into the tree wildly, each thud followed by a pained growl.

Then he turns to us, and the vacant expression is back. Blood coats half his face, dripping from his crooked nose and the cut on his forehead.

He throws the sword at me, but I push it off course with a wind blast. It sticks harmlessly into the ground behind me.

Seath runs at Kiran with an animalistic fury, pummeling him as he snarls and growls like a beast, beating him near-unconscious in only a few seconds before turning to me.

"Kiran!" I cry out.

Without meaning to, I summon giants from all three of our shadows, and they attempt to restrain Seath as Kiran meekly stumbles back and collapses against a tree. Celly flies to his side and begins trying to heal him.

I can't freeze the monster without hurting Seath, his body is reinforced against direct attacks, and clearly restraining him won't be easy, as he has already torn two of my giants apart with his bare hands.

But perhaps I could fry the monster. As the last giant falls, I fire a sustained bolt of weak lightning into him. The constant shock slows his movements, and he writhes in pain.

He drops to his hands and knees. I can see his fist close around something, but I don't realize what until the ball of mud hits me right in the eyes. I yelp and recoil, trying to wipe it from my face, but the second I clear it out, he's upon me. He picks me up over his head and throws me against the ground next to his sword.

I pull myself up to my knees as he pulls the blade free from the ground. He grabs a fistful of my hair, knocking my hat free, and I start to scream, but my voice cuts out when I feel the sharp tip of the blade press against my chest.

His hand is shaking.

I look up at his face. His expression is vacant, but I can see tears forming in his eyes. My hair falls through his loosening grip, and he stares down at me.

With his face unchanged, he spins the sword in his hand and presses the tip against his own abdomen.

"No!" I cry, latching onto his arm. "Please! I know I can save you! I'm begging you, please trust me!"

I feel Kiran slump against me from behind and he, too, grabs Seath's arm. "You better not be giving up on us . . . Yukiko's mad dog doesn't lose so easily!"

Cara jumps on his back, clenching both arms under his chin. "Nobody wants you to sacrifice yourself, you stubborn jerk!"

He begins to lower the blade, but then, despite us holding him back with all our strength, he sinks the sword into himself—right through his leg, just above the knee.

He lets out a beastly, pained scream and throws Kiran and I back. He grabs Cara's arm and pulls her free of his back and throws her into us as he collapses on his good knee, his injured leg awkwardly jutting out straight in front of him.

He then smashes his hands against a nearby large rock, bending all his fingers back and breaking them at once.

"What's he doing?!" Cara shrieks.

"Seath!" I shout.

He shakes his head and returns his attention to us, but with the blade stuck in his leg he cannot get up, and with his mangled hands he cannot pull it free.

"He's protecting us," Kiran says breathlessly. "He disabled his leg and his hands so the thing possessing him couldn't make him hurt us."

Cara wipes tears from her eyes. "We have to save him, but how? Anything we do to hurt the monster will inevitably hurt him too, right?"

"Correct," Celly states. "And we do not have much time. I estimate that he will experience exsanguination in nine minutes."

"What does that mean?" Cara asks.

But as I look at the stream of scarlet running down the blade, I understand. With a horrified tremor in my voice, I say, "He's bleeding out."

What can we do though? How can we save him?

A man whose body is awake while his mind sleeps is lost in his dreams

It couldn't be, could it? I look around the shore, and sure enough, there it is, resting on the grass near the shore, where he first attacked us. Seath's grimoire. I call it to my hands with air magic and quickly begin flipping through the pages under the "mind" tab.

"What are you doing?" Kiran asks. "Nine minutes isn't a lot of time, you know!"

"Eight minutes now," Celly adds.

There it is. The circle Seath once used to explore my dreams and see what I was seeing.

"I'm going to enter his dreams and help him restore control from the inside," I say as I copy the spell over to my grimoire.

"Will that work?" Cara asks.

"I hope so."

I walk toward Seath, staying just out of range, and close my eyes, drawing all the strength that I have. And with a deep breath, I invoke the dreamcatcher-style array, connecting my mind to his.

XVII.

The Boy

I stand among clouds as if atop an invisible plane, as torrential rain drenches me. I hear a voice on the wind, but it's so faint I can't make it out. Ahead of me is a door, floating ominously in the air. The faded brown paint is peeling, and the door frame is worse for wear. The knocker just above the peephole is broken, and the brass on the doorknob has faded to green.

I turn the knob and the wind whips the door open with a heavy thud, revealing a dark, decrepit townhouse.

" . . . Mom?" a voice whispers from beyond.

I step inside, and the door closes behind me with a thud. Everything stinks of cigarettes and mold. Just across the entry threshold is the living room, with only a beaten-up couch and a recliner facing an old tube TV playing static. There's a boy, no older than eight or nine, shaking the arm of the woman in the chair. They have the same unkempt brown hair.

"Mom, why won't you get up?" the boy asks tearfully, shaking her more. As I step closer, I notice her skin has a grey hue, and her brown eyes have a glassy, empty look as she stares at nothing in particular. She's perfectly still.

She's not breathing.

With a mighty crack of thunder everything is gone, and now the boy and I are in an alley, in some strange city. His clothes are drab and tattered and filthy, and he seems far too thin.

"Little boy?" I call.

He turns to look at me with those familiar mismatched eyes—one brown, one blue.

This isn't a dream he's trapped in. It's a nightmare.

"Juniper," Seath whispers, looking at me. "Juniper, what are you doing here?"

"I'm Selena, don't you recognize me?" I ask. "I need you to wake up, Seath, something's controlling you in the real world and you need to wake up."

Thunder cracks and Seath jumps, peering past me in terror. "She's coming."

The ground begins to tremble as the thunder beckons the heavy steps of some terrible monster. A great cloud of black smoke with a woman's upper body glides into view in the street beyond the alley. She is as tall as a building, with long hair and massive, blindingly bright eyes of television static.

Seath runs scared in the other direction, so I give chase. As I look over my shoulder, the woman lets out an inhuman shriek and begins following menacingly.

I start to hear disembodied voices in my head whispering *murderer* over and over again, like some sort of ritualistic chant.

I catch up to the young Seath, and for a moment, everything goes dark.

Then we're in a hallway that seems to go on forever in either direction. The monster is gone, and it's just me and him.

"What is this place?" I ask.

He looks out the window, and following his gaze, I see another building through the rain and fog. It's a house with bars on the windows that looks as if it doesn't belong here. It's an eerie, sad-looking place, poorly taken care of and more indicative of a prison than a family home.

There is a flash of lightning and the whispers start up again. Through the fog the monster returns, climbing over the house as it dissolves into nothing.

"June, come on!" Seath says, grabbing my wrist and running down the hall.

The monster stays in step with us through the infinite hall, staring menacingly at us as we run. Then she swipes the side of the building, tearing the wall down. Her form flies into the hole and appears stuffed

160

uncomfortably in our path, but when we turn to run the other way, she's behind us, too.

I look out through the destroyed wall. The ground is gone now—there is nothing but void below. But it doesn't seem like we have much choice. I pick Seath up and leap through the tear, falling into the fog below.

Our descent slows and we drift among clouds, as if in zero gravity.

"Who is that monster?" I ask him.

He shakes his head tearfully. "I can't say. I can't!"

Something in my heart breaks for him. He's just a scared little boy in here. How much of this is the monster terrorizing him, and how much is him terrorizing himself? How do I wake him up?

"Can you take me anywhere, Seath?" I ask. "This is your mind, after all."

"But every time we jump, I get closer to *that place*, and no matter where we go she'll find us!"

I squeeze his small hand. "It'll be okay. Just once more. Please."

If there is any light to be found in his dream world, that would be the place, I'm sure of it.

He nods, and we land in a snow-filled field. There is a path following the bank of a river, and on the other side of the path is a trail of transmission towers. On the other side of the river is a hill with a tree, where a silhouetted figure sits.

Seath walks to the edge of the river, and I notice a trail of stones just breaching the water's surface, forming a precarious pathway. I can see the real memory in my mind as clear as I see him now standing there. It comes to me as if it were my own—Seath as a young adult, tall, fit, and without a beard, stops at the rocks. He jumps from rock to rock to get to the other side, but slips at the very last one, falling in. Yukiko sets her book down and gracefully walks down the hill, and as he steps out of the river, she smiles at him and asks if he is okay.

Where is this place? It's not Kalpana. It may not even be America.

Seath fidgets with his hands as he watches the rocks.

"Aren't you going?" I say to the little boy.

"I want to, but I'm scared," he says. "If I cross the river, I'll have to go to that place again."

The clouds above grow dark, and the rain begins to fall. Lightning and thunder announce the return of the cloud monster, who looms ominously over us on our side of the river.

"Go!" I tell him. No more running.

"You can't beat her!" he says.

"Just get across!" I yell back.

The monster swipes at me, but I summon a windstorm to my hands and blast the shadows back.

Murderer, the voices on the wind whisper as the monster reforms herself. I continue to blast her, but she keeps coming back bigger and bigger, until her body almost completely envelops this side of the river.

I follow Seath across the rocks, and he runs to the tree, but Yukiko's silhouette is gone. I catch up to him as the monster closes in.

My senses tell me there is no magical presence in the monster, which must mean that it's a figment of Seath's nightmare, and not the thing keeping him here. But then what is?

"Seath, what is the place you don't want to go to?" I ask on a hunch.

He sits and hugs his knees to his chest. "The bad place."

"That's right, what is the bad place?"

He shakes his head. "It's where she comes from."

"Take me there!"

"I can't! I can't go there, I can't! Please don't make me, June," he sobs.

I kneel in front of him and put my hands on his shoulders. "It's okay to be scared. But we have to go there. I don't know what's waiting for us, but I promise

I'll be right here, just like you're always there for me outside of this nightmare. Okay?"

He looks into my eyes and I can see the terror gripping him.

Everything disappears, even Seath. I find myself alone in the dark for a moment, until the familiar patter of rain begins to fall on me. I look around, and I am on a beach at night, near some cliffs. The sea is rough and choppy, and there is a torrential storm.

I know this place. I feel like I've been here before. As I look at the cliffs, then out to sea, it dawns on me. I have dreamt of this beach before. Yukiko and Cyra fought against each other just over the sea here.

Nearby, I hear the sounds of fighting. It's dark, but I can just make out two men trading magical blows. I can hear the grunts and shouts as they clash.

A spectral force suddenly bursts from my body, causing me to nearly stumble. The strange force takes the shape of a short, black-haired girl of twelve with red eyes. She looks just like Yukiko.

In the distance I hear a woman's voice shrieking, and as I follow the little girl toward the men, I realize the fight is already over.

"Seath!" the little girl whimpers.

He looks just as he did in my dream of Cyra and Yukiko here. He stands over the crumpled form of a man with an ice claw cast over his left hand, and the claw drips ruby.

He looks back at the small girl and his eyes widen. "Juniper? You're here?"

"No!" a woman screams, rushing to the fallen man's side. The woman from the lake, and from my dreams, the witch who has been stalking me. It's her.

"What have you done?" she cries, cradling the fallen man in her arms.

Lightning strikes the beach and takes Yukiko's form. Seath dismisses his claws and takes a step toward the little girl, but she runs to Yukiko and clings to her white cloak, hiding behind her.

From afar, Cyra appears with three other women behind her, their faces obscured in the storm. One, the smallest of them all, in a black cloak and a masquerade mask, lets out a guttural scream and lunges toward Seath, but Cyra holds her back.

"I'll kill you!" the woman shouts.

"Velia!" Cyra commands as she restrains her comrade. "Yukiko's mad dog will still be here tomorrow, but for now, our sister needs us."

The masked woman, Velia, relents, and kneels beside the crying witch, rubbing her shoulders.

"[illegible]," Seath says her name, but for some reason I can't hear it. It sounds jumbled, like an audio clip that has been distorted. "I didn't mean to, it was an accident."

"We will back off for now," Yukiko says regretfully. "Mourn him in peace."

The crying witch looks up at Seath and says just one word. "*Murderer.*"

With a flash of lightning, everyone is gone, and it is now day. The ocean is calm, and there is a breeze. The little boy form of Seath appears again at my side.

"She was right the whole time, wasn't she?" I ask him as I watch the horizon. "You really did murder someone."

"Her husband," he replies. "It was an accident, I didn't mean to do it. I was just trying to protect Yukiko."

"You were afraid of me finding out? Because you thought I would look at you the way that young girl did?" I ask.

"You never looked at me the same after that, June."

"Seath, you're the one trapping yourself in this nightmare. I need you to wake up for me."

"But if I wake up, you'll be gone," he replies. "Yukiko will be gone, too, and then it will be just me."

"But it isn't just you. We're all here, and we need you. Everyone's fighting to save you," I tell him.

A look of realization dawns on him. "You're not Juniper."

I can feel something drawing me away from the dream. Everything starts to go white, and I hear something whisper— "Selena."

I am back at the lake with Cara, Kiran, and Celly. I stumble back from Seath, clutching my head. I study his vacant expression for a moment until, finally, he begins blinking and growing aware. He opens his mouth to say something, but then he groans and looks away, vomiting up a shrimp-like water monster.

I freeze the monster, and Celly blasts it with a fire bolt, destroying it once and for all.

The threat is gone but we're not out of the woods yet. Seath weakly lies back, his skin starting to turn a sickly grey color. I rush to his side and flip through my grimoire to the wound-healing spell. I don't have to call for Cara or Celly, they both follow my lead without a word.

The three of us combine our magic and pour it into Seath. He grimaces and grinds his teeth, and I can see his jaw clench with each sickening snap as the bones in his hands pull themselves back to their original shape. His cuts begin to scab and close rapidly, leaving only his leg.

"Kiran–"

"Way ahead of you," he interrupts, gripping the sword's handle. "Sorry, Seath."

Seath squeezes around his injured leg with a grim expression, his eyes locked on Kiran. "Just do it."

I can't watch. I look away the second I see Kiran pull. But even the squelching noises and Seath's agonizing howls are enough to leave me nauseous. I can't help but give in to the urge to look, just as he jerks the blade free.

"It's out!" Kiran shouts, and I focus all of my remaining strength on sealing the wound. With the bleeding stopped, all of us drop, sitting as comfortably as we can on the ground. Seath wheezes, lying flat on his back. Celly returns to my hands. I close my eyes for a moment and listen to the sounds of everyone breathing, relief washing over me. He's going to be okay.

"What a day," Seath finally whispers.

A freezing-cold hand weakly envelops mine, and I open my eyes to see Seath rolled over on his side, reaching for me. His expression is neutral, but he squeezes my hand and says, "Thank you."

I cannot tell if the words came from him, or the little boy from his nightmares. Perhaps, at this moment, there isn't a difference.

XVIII.
The Workshop

Seath lays sprawled on the couch, wincing in pain as Cara's mom inspects the wound on his left leg. Cara, Kiran, Celly, and I watch from the other couch. There is a mix of both relief and anxiety in the air.

"Quit fussing," Mrs. Philomena commands.

"Do you have any idea how much that hurts?" he groans.

"If you wanted painkillers you should have gone to the hospital. And no, forty ounces of bourbon when you have children in your care doesn't count," she retorts sternly. "Just because I'm an RN does not mean I can be a substitute for the ER."

"How is he?" I ask tentatively.

"Well there's a lot to be said for healing magic, I'll grant you that," she replies, letting out a sigh. "At the very least his life isn't in danger. But there is significant damage to the leg. He needs to go to a hospital and get tests done, but if I had to guess, I'd say this is going to be permanent. How bad it ends up being is up to him."

"What do you mean?" Seath makes a pained face as he adjusts himself.

Mrs Philomena points at his leg. "I mean if you don't start taking better care of yourself as of *yesterday*, your leg is going to be a paperweight by March. If you want to keep some function in it, you need to start taking care of your body."

Seath sighs. "Alright, be specific."

"For starters you are going to a hospital, end of story," she says, crossing her arms. "If you can't make the walk to my car, you'll be going in an ambulance. And when we get you home, no more sleeping on the couch. Are you out of your mind? You're over sixty, do you have any idea how bad that is for your back?"

"I haven't been able to sleep in the master bedroom in thirty years, it's—"

"You're going to have to get over that. Would you rather be in a wheelchair? Hm?" she says sternly. "And another thing, you're going to cut way back on the junk food and alcohol. Eat something green and stop getting stabbed, and you might just live to see seventy."

"Good lord," Seath complains. "Like mother, like daughter! Alright already, I get it. I'll relocate to the bedroom after we get home."

Kiran leans forward, his elbows resting on his knees. "There is a fifth bedroom, right? If it's too hard for you to sleep in Yukiko's room for . . . emotional reasons, you could stay there."

He shakes his head. "I don't exactly think I'd be comfortable in there, either. There's some history there. Besides, the bed is way too small."

Cara and her mom excuse themselves for a few moments to talk and catch up. I nod to Kiran, and he takes Celly and gives me and Seath some space, too.

Seath struggles to sit up, trying to keep his injured leg straight. I look at the cane resting on the table. Despite cleaning it, I don't think I'll ever get the mental picture of Kiran pulling it free from his leg out of my mind.

That's not the only thing from today I can't get out of my head.

"I know what you're thinking," Seath says finally. "The fact that Kiran can't remember the identity of Cyra's comrade either proves that our memories are being blocked by some kind of spell."

"There has to be some kind of counter-spell or something, a way for us to get rid of that block," I reply.

He shakes his head. "Magic that manipulates the mind can be tricky. It takes a lot of focus and power, and sometimes you just can't make it work. People with a strong magical constitution like Yukiko were pretty much immune to this type of thing, but Kiran and I have no magic to speak of, and clearly we both have some unresolved issues around Cyra and her companions. That makes us vulnerable."

"Can you remember who the man was?" I press.

"He was her consort and husband, Al." His eyes drop, and he anxiously runs his fingers through his hair for a moment. "It was an accident. You have to know I didn't mean for him to die. The adrenaline rush was crazy, and I couldn't see Yukiko anymore. I was desperate to find her and make sure she was safe, and he just kept attacking me, and I just swung."

I hesitate before I ask, unsure if I even want to know. "How many . . ."

"Three," he says quietly. "I've killed three men. Al, and two of Cyra's vassals. Al was the first, though, and his death escalated everything."

A silence grows between us, stretching on for long moments. If someone killed Seath the way he killed Al, I would hate them too. I don't know what to think. He seems to regret it, but that doesn't change the past. Maybe it really was just a mistake? Would I have done anything differently in that situation? Will this fight with Cyra and her allies make me a killer too?

Into the silence I ask, "Who is Juniper?"

His face grows dark as if recalling a distant, painful memory. "Maybe in the future, I'll tell you all about her."

There is an air of melancholy in the house for the next while. Seath is in and out of the house attending doctors' appointments and getting his knee looked after, and Cara, Celly, Kiran, and I are left to our own devices.

We won, but we're still no closer to figuring out the identity of the witch attacking us. And as long as we remain in the dark, she can keep coming after us until she wins. We need to put a stop to this.

From turning my friends against me to manipulating Seath and Kiran's memories, it feels like we have been totally outplayed from the start, but there must be someone who can help identify her.

I wander the house alone one evening and follow the upstairs hallway to the left instead of the right. Sure enough, there is another bedroom like Seath said, though it's locked. The room next door feels like some kind of museum of weapons, and across the hall is a large music and art room, though everything has been covered in pale sheets.

There is just one more unfamiliar room. The tower room.

It has Yukiko's sigil on the door, and as I turn the knob, my own sigil activates. It feels like I am breaking through invisible glass as I push the door open. So it was locked with some kind of magic, probably designed to only respond to the powers of the moon.

The room itself is nothing special—there is a workbench, a drafting desk, a handful of bookshelves, and a chalkboard. In the middle of the room, a spiral staircase leads up.

I inspect the desk and find it full of writing and drawing supplies. The workbench is weathered and littered with woodworking tools and old shavings. I pick up a large, square book from the shelf and sit it on the workbench, opening it up and flipping through. There are all kinds of circles inside and notes, all written by hand instead of with the copying spell.

Inside, I find a diagram of a body in a room, with a different circle on each wall, including on the ceiling and floor. The next page shows a diagram of a human body with different magic circles marked on the forehead, the chest, the stomach, each hand, each thigh, each foot, and on the backside, one on each shoulder blade, a small one just above the butt, and a large array on the back.

It seems like Yukiko was working on something very complex in here. Her notes are technical and difficult to understand, but a particular passage stands out;

> *The spirit is toxic, and cannot be bound to a container for which it was not originally made. Human souls bound to other objects will rot them, eventually destroying the container. Even if the container was made to be an exact replica of the original body, or infused with the bones of the original, once recalled from death, the spirit will reject its shell. Indeed, once the spirit leaves the original body, even if repaired, it will be rejected.*

The doll still seems to be the best way forward. I must find Jack and Saira.

I turn from the book and my curiosity takes me upstairs. As I reach the top and look around, I recoil and let out a gasp.

For a moment it's like Yukiko is standing right in front of me, but upon closer inspection, it's a wooden mannequin made in her likeness. And that's not the only one. I recognize the damaged Lyra mannequin as well, still missing an arm and severely damaged, and there are many others, too, that look generic.

The naked dolls all have strange circles painted on their bodies, not too unlike the image from the book, but the dolls have fewer circles and different arrays. I frown. Just what was she planning? Was she trying to bring herself back to life?

I think back to how it felt to live inside the body of the doll Lyra. It's an uneasy feeling, to see her broken, cracked shell sitting limp against the wall. This is the only doll without magic circles on her body - perhaps the spells were used up when I inhabited it?

"Hello?" Seath's voice calls from below. "We both know I'm not making it up those stairs, so come down."

I turn to leave, but I stop on the first stair and turn back to Yukiko's doll, an idea forming in my head. As I make my way down to Seath, I turn it over in my mind.

"What are you doing in here?" he asks.

176

"I have an idea for how we can figure out who's been attacking us," I tell him. "Yukiko knew their identities, and she's not affected by the memory spell, so let's go back in time and ask her."

XIX.
Lost In Memory

"Would it work?" Kiran asks as we sit around the table in the library.

Seath sighs. "Technically, yes. But you don't know what you're dealing with here. Time is one of the primordial forces, like death and space. I told you once before, didn't I? The harder you push against the natural laws of the universe, the harder the universe pushes back. And there is nothing the universe hates more than people who try to cheat time."

"What would we need to try it?" Cara asks.

"It would take multiple powerful spells, at least two people, a pathway, and an anchor to even attempt this," he answers.

"We know it's possible because Yukiko did it. She pulled me back in time to save me from Cyra," I say.

"A: That was a very specific situation, with very specific circumstances, that Yukiko prepared utilizing her powers as a seer," Seath says. "And B: Yukiko was a lot more experienced than you. If you mess this up you could get lost in time forever, or you could die."

"If we don't figure out who this woman is, we could die, too," Cara points out.

Celly flies from my side to address the table. "All we need to break the memory spell is either a photo of her, or her name, isn't that right?"

"The only place you'll find photos is at Cyra's home, though, and it's a fortress," Kiran explains.

I nod. "We'll definitely die if we go there."

"So let's try going back to Yukiko's time," Cara says.

We take the day off school, and Seath gives us each multiple magic circles to copy, and goes over the instructions in detail. One mistake could cost us everything, so it will come down to Cara and I.

We prepare a ritual space outside once the moon is high, using salt to create an eight-pointed star at the base of the yew tree. At each point there is a ceramic bowl, each filled respectively with dirt, fresh water, ground herbs, sticks and leaves set on fire, a piece of silver, various seeds, and a wax candle.

Cara and I kneel over the eighth and final bowl as Seath takes his cane sword from the sheath and pricks our fingers. The two of us squeeze a few drops into the bowl. Then Cara undoes the top couple of buttons of her shirt, and sighs.

"This part is going to be gross," she mutters.

"I think drawing the circle is going to be worse," I retort.

"No, wearing your blood is definitely worse!"

I can't argue with that. With my bleeding finger I draw a circle with a triangle inside, and a triskeles pattern in the center. Cara takes her place by the tree, and I take mine in the center of the star array.

I take Yukiko's ring off and keep it in my left hand.

"You can only try this once," Seath warns. "Once you do, the yew tree's magical connection to Yukiko will be spent, and the door to the past closed forever. The yew tree is your path, it is an object of nature with a lot of spiritual energy that can lead to Yukiko's time. Cara is your anchor, the circle on her chest will be used to recall your soul from the past. You two know what you have to do?"

Cara and I nod to each other.

"Just so you know," Seath says, "I've never actually seen anyone do this successfully, but from what I've read, it's gonna suck. Brace yourselves, and begin when you're ready."

Cara and I take a deep breath, then we invoke the eight-pointed star array together. We cast the spells over each of the bowls one by one, each draining our energy dramatically. Even only after four, the power it takes to sustain them has me feeling faint. One by one we connect to the last four, until only the blood bowl is left.

When we cast the spell over the blood bowl, my entire body immediately feels like it has been set on fire. Cara screams, sharing in my pain, but she forces herself to maintain composure. Finally, I project one last circle on my own—the centerpiece being a wireframe-like array in the shape of a twisted hourglass. It appears right on the trunk of the tree.

All of the sudden, I feel myself being drawn into the center of the circle, even though my body remains right where it is. My spirit is pulled free of my body, and I am drawn through what feels like a tunnel. I can feel each circle draining my power—my mind feels like it's fracturing. I clutch Yukiko's ring as hard as I can and use my senses to guide me all the way through to the other side of the tunnel.

Just like last time, the yew tree is gone and the house looks more vibrant. The weather is nice, and there is a spring breeze in the morning air.

At the end of the driveway, I can see a young Seath playing with Yukiko's white wolf as if the great beast were just an ordinary dog. He repeatedly throws a large stick into the woods for the dog to chase, and rewards him with globes of ice to cool down with.

"They say that the person whom your familiar spirit is most affectionate with is the one you are destined to be with," Yukiko says from behind me. I turn around, and there she is, dressed casually in a long sky-blue skirt down to her ankles and a white sweater. "I daresay my beloved Tsuki has put her trust in the right man."

"I–"

"We shouldn't disturb their peace while they can enjoy it. It seems like a trivial thing when every day the world feels like it is coming to an end, but you must always remember to find time for joy."

I try to speak but everything around me disappears and I am suddenly in the garden. It's now warm—within seconds beads of sweat start to form on my brow and the back of my neck, and the sun is blinding. It is evidently mid-day.

I spot Yukiko walking among the beautiful array of flowers of all colors and types, wearing a thin white summer dress and a wide-brimmed straw hat.

"Yukiko? Please listen to me, I need your help," I plead.

A green moth flutters around me, landing on a beautiful white rose just below the big library windows.

"A rose is a rather aggressive symbol for love, don't you think? The blooms are intricate and powerful and demand to be noticed, yet if you are not careful the thorns will hurt you," she says wistfully. "And yet isn't that a measure of true love, to appreciate the bloom in spite of the thorns?"

I am transported once more to the lake at dusk. The leaves have all changed color, and thousands of them have fallen from their respective trees and adorned the still waters of the lake, like flakes of gold and ruby.

Yukiko stands at the edge of the lake, dipping her toes in the water in a belted, blue sweater dress. On the branch above her is her great owl, watching me carefully as I approach.

"It's okay, Yuki," she coos. "Our visitor is quite harmless."

"I need you to tell me the names of the witches who fight for Cyra Oralie, please," I beg. "One of them cast a spell so nobody can remember who she is, so we can't track her or defend against her. I need your help!"

"Have you ever wondered why we cannot use magic to empower others without weakening ourselves?" she asks aimlessly. "Why is it that this great gift requires so much sacrifice to master? Is it to teach us humility?"

"I don't know, is that important right now?"

"We witches hoard our power, sharing it only with the ones we love most and our devoted subjects, but perhaps all along the true purpose of our gifts was to share them," she says. "The ability to do so, is that not what truly makes us special?"

As the world begins to change again, I shout, "Wait!"

I appear in the library this time. It's night, and Yukiko is alone, her chair facing the window. There is snow outside, and a storm rattles the glass.

"Welcome, Moonchild," she says.

There is something different about her, as she sits in her witch's outfit in the light of the moon. Physically, she is unchanged, but I sense a weakness and frailty in her.

I walk up to her chair and stand beside her. "This is when you die, isn't it?"

"Tomorrow evening, right in this very chair," she replies matter-of-factly.

"Aren't you scared?"

"Of course, but everything that lives must eventually die. All stories must end." She tips her head towards me. "Even yours, someday."

"Can you see that far in the future?" I ask anxiously.

She shakes her head. "The future is never certain. That's what makes it worth fighting for. No matter how dark it may seem, there is always hope."

"Why won't you tell me who's responsible for what's going on in my time?"

Her frosty lips curl into a big smile. "I would have thought that was obvious, my dear Moonchild. You already know. The answer waits for you where it has always been—in your dreams."

I feel myself being pulled right out of reality. I desperately try to resist, but my spirit is yanked from the past and drawn toward Cara.

Everything goes blank, and when I open my eyes I am back in front of the yew. I gasp for air and start coughing, clutching my chest to try and settle my thumping heart.

"Selena!" Cara rushes to my side.

I look at my hands and notice my skin has a greyish hue, and I feel chilled to the bone. I have no strength in my legs, and I lean on Cara for support.

"Is she okay?" Kiran asks, helping Cara support me.

Seath steps in front of me and grabs my chin, forcing me to face him. "Her spirit was detached from her body for almost an hour. She should be okay with some rest, but it's a good thing we pulled her out. Any longer, and her body might have died before she could return to it."

"Here," Kiran says, picking me up. I weakly wrap my arms around him for support and lean my head against his shoulder as he carries me to my bed.

I can't bring myself to even open my eyes as he places me down. I can hear his voice, talking to the others, but I can't make out what they are saying. Instead, I drift off to sleep, in search of answers.

XX.

What the Storm Brings

As I find myself back in the dream, I look at the clock. Four. My hands ball into fists. I'm tired of letting this person control my life and hurt my friends without consequence. This stops now.

I fire a wind blast that shatters the clock, and I summon my grimoire to my hand. This is my dream. I call the shots here, not her.

I climb on top of the railing and look out toward the school where she stands, and I close my eyes. I let myself fall forward, over the edge, and in mid-air I summon my wings and rapidly soar towards her.

Geysers burst from beneath the ground, firing in my path, but I dodge them. Out of the corner of my eye I watch streams of water trace their way along the tops of buildings. The streams wrap around weak points in the structure and superheat until they burst, sending chunks of debris down to crush me.

As I get closer, the sea serpent bursts forth from the sea above, but I keep my focus singularly on the witch. I empower my fist and fly at her as fast as possible, letting my speed carry the momentum of my fist right into her. A barrier of water intercepts my punch, absorbing and dispersing the energy through the waves.

She grips the sword on her hip, a ninjatō, and I can't help but notice the silver ring on her finger. I can't help but think I've seen it before, with the same teardrop diamond and everything.

Something in my senses is screaming at me to turn around, so I look over my shoulder. The great sea snake is flying at me, jaw unhinged, ready to swallow me whole. As the jaws close in around me, I wake up cozy in bed, sometime just before sunrise.

Yukiko was right. I have known all along where to find her.

"Celly," I call, and they fly up to my face to greet me.

"Selena! You're awake. Everyone was starting to worry," they say. "You've been sleeping for thirty-two hours straight."

Hearing her say it makes me hyper-aware of how dry my throat feels, and the dull ache in my stomach. I drag myself out of bed to the shower, and come out of the bathroom with my witch outfit on.

"Gather everyone downstairs," I tell Celly. "I know where the witch is!"

I head to the foyer to wait for everyone. Cara and Celly arrive first, then Kiran, helping Seath slowly get down the stairs.

"You should be resting," Seath huffs through his groans of pain. "You just traveled back in time, take another day."

"We don't have time. I know where the witch is right now, and if we don't go after her and she realizes what we know, we could miss our chance!" I tell them.

"So Yukiko told you?" Seath asks.

I shake my head. "No, but she told me how to find the answer. She's at the school."

"Hold on, it's a weekend," Kiran says. "She won't be there."

"The school is open on Sundays for some athletics, remedial lessons, and the night school program, according to their official website," Celly tells us.

"We can't just charge in without a plan," Cara says.

"We need to be careful, this is a powerful opponent," Seath adds.

"What if we didn't fight her?" Kiran suggests. "All we have to do is identify her, and then we can back off. We'll catch her off guard, so we'll have the upper hand."

There is a silent tension in the air for a moment as Seath thinks it over, but eventually he relents. "Alright, but we don't stay. We fall back immediately, okay? Even four on one she will be a powerful enemy, and a cornered beast is the most dangerous of all. Everyone do what you need to do to prepare."

At Seath's insistence, Cara and I both eat a bit to help recover our strength.

With Seath in tow, we make our way across town. Due to his injured leg, our progress is slow, and as we walk, the rain starts to fall. By the time our group reaches the school, it has become a downpour, and all of us are drenched as we walk in through the front doors. Just as Celly said, it's open.

I search my senses for any sign of magic, but I can't find anything. So I look at the first place I can think of, the place where the witch always appears in my dreams—the rooftop.

We make our way to the stairs and follow them all the way to the top, finding the door surprisingly unlocked. As we open it and walk into the rain once more, a tingling sensation creeps up my spine. Something, somewhere, some spell, is activating.

"I can feel something," I tell the others, looking around.

Seath jams the door so it doesn't close automatically, then limps closer. "What is it?"

"It's like something is waking up. Some kind of spell. I can't exactly place it, but it might mean she's on to us."

Suddenly, something compels me to look back at the doorway we came from. Celly and Cara both seem fixated on it as well.

Sure enough, we can hear the sound of footsteps, and a familiar face rises from the stairwell.

"Not you," Cara whispers in shock as Ms. Rivers stands in the doorway, clutching a strange blue book with bronze designs on it.

"Oh dear, what gave me away?" Ms. Rivers says with a coy grin.

"Your ring," I tell her. "I kept having prophetic visions of you in my dreams, and I realized why my dream kept placing you here, at the school, when I saw your ring."

"You're the one who I met in the road that night, the night before I was possessed. I remember now, I saw you at the end of the driveway when I had the dog out," Seath says.

"All this time you've been attacking us?" Cara says, scowling through her tears.

"She's using a glamor, a spell to obfuscate her appearance," Kiran says. "That's why we couldn't recognize you. You preyed on the fact that Seath and I had both lost our powers, didn't you?"

She reaches up to her blouse and begins undoing the top buttons slowly, then with a wave of her hand, her sigil appears on her chest, hidden with magic.

"You certainly have a knack for complicating things, you and your little scooby gang of misfits," she says mockingly. "Had you died when you were supposed to, this would be over by now, but your stubbornness is endless. Now, all of your friends will die with you."

"It's still four on one," I bark back.

"Five," Seath says, unsheathing his cane sword. "Injury or no injury, I'm not leaving the fighting just to you kids."

"Oh, Seath," she says. "This is a private party, and I'm afraid you're not invited. But don't worry, I'll pay you the same courtesy you paid me when you murdered Alton Rivers. I'll let you collect their bodies."

The water pooling under all of us from the rain springs to life, forming bubbles around all of us except Seath. The last thing I see is a look of terror on his face before the world outside the bubbles disappears in a flash, and we are transported to a familiar beach.

"Where are we?" Cara shouts.

"We appear to be somewhere on the west coast," Celly clarifies.

Kiran points to something far away in the wild and choppy sea. "What is that?"

As the monster from my dreams bursts from the depths of the sea and reveals his colossal size on the horizon, panic starts to set in.

I finally understand the nature of this magic. It is a power connected to water, to storms, and to illusions. It is the power of the deep, and all the terrifying monsters that dwell within, like that great sea serpent.

She is the Witch of the Seas, and we are now in her domain.

XXI.

Leviathan

The sea serpent unveils his whole mighty body with a flourish, flying through the air on the horizon as if challenging us to face him.

Cara drops her bag and retrieves her quiver from inside, then summons her bow and Kiran's sword.

"Well, it's a good thing I brought extra arrows, isn't it?" she says glibly, though the tremble in her voice betrays her attempt to act unafraid.

"Fighting this enemy without aerial capabilities will be impossible," Celly says. "It would be prudent to share your flying spell with Cara."

I let her copy the spell from my grimoire, and the two of us create our wings—mine resembling a monarch butterfly, while hers resemble green transparent fairy wings.

The monster sends a tsunami our way. I look at Kiran, who grips his sword and looks frustrated. "I'm sorry, but since you can't fly–"

I cast a shadow bubble around him as Cara, Celly, and I take to the skies to avoid the wave crashing into the beach.

The beast comes toward us at great speed and lunges, jaw agape. Celly launches a firebolt down his throat and we all fly in different directions to avoid him.

Cara's ice arrows seem to do nothing but bounce off of the monster's iron-like exterior. I try to freeze him by calling down the stars, but even two dozen beams at once aren't enough to slow him down. He moves incredibly fast, shrugging off all of our attacks, and repeatedly lunging at me.

If ice won't work, then maybe another element? I call down powerful storms of lightning from above to strike the beast, but they are ineffective. Maybe I need to be more direct. How can we beat something this huge?

I watch as Cara flies high above the beast and notches an arrow to her bow, taking aim at the beast. The arrow flies, bringing with it the force of a hurricane, straight into the beast's skull. The monster, unphased, turns to face her and fires off a high-pressure jet of water from his throat. I can sense Cara throwing up a barrier in time, but the force pushes her far away.

We can't keep this up forever. I'm so relieved she was able to defend herself in time, but eventually someone will get hurt if we don't do something. I need to think. They're depending on me.

I create a lightning blade and try to attack the monster, but his scales are too hard and the blade keeps harmlessly bouncing off. I need to get through his armor to hurt him—I need another way of getting around it.

I need a blade that can pass through his armor. A blade that won't cut, and thus won't bounce off. A blade that can reach where he's most vulnerable. With my sigil, I spawn a blade of ethereal magic in my hand that is intangible to everything except me. As the great sea serpent coils in mid-air and tries to swallow me whole, I narrowly dodge in mid-air and swing the sword through his body, freezing his insides.

As I pull the sword away I notice his tail just as it whips into me, sending me crashing towards the beach, knocking the air from my lungs. I tumble head over heels in the air, trying and failing to catch my breath. Disoriented, I can't even tell which way is up.

A burst of air presses into my back, slowing my momentum. Then another. And another. Celly comes into view beside me as I half-crash, half-land in the sand, the world spinning around me as I try and fail to take a full breath.

The monster stalks over to the beach and looms menacingly over me. My knees go limp and my hands tremble as I take in the truly terrifying size of the great beast. As he slowly leans down, opening his maw, Kiran runs between us, sword in hand, and my heart skips a beat. Seath's words echo in my head:

"For someone like Kiran, it goes against every instinct in his body to not throw himself between you and danger."

I'm too drained. I can't win like this, and neither can Kiran—but I can't let him die standing between me and my enemies either.

I struggle to stand, stumbling to my knees on the first attempt. The monster opens his mouth wide, and I can already hear the gurgling, rushing sound of water inside his throat.

I don't know what to do, but I have to do something. I search within myself, saying *'please'* in my head as if asking the Moon itself to guide me, to tell me what to do, to save me. Save us.

On instinct I throw my arms around Kiran, my left palm pressed against his chest, and I burrow my face in his back. I can feel his heart pounding as if trying to leap into my palm. I can sense an unbreakable determination in him as he stands in defiance of death and the monster who threatens it. My sigil tingles as I feel a deepening sense of connection between us, and I whisper into his back, "I need you."

I close my eyes tightly and press my palm more firmly into his chest, and I imagine myself placing every ounce of strength I have left into him, and his heart accepting it without a moment's hesitation.

A thunderous crash jolts me from my trance, and I can see a shield of ice intercepting the monster's water blast.

Kiran steps out of my reach and looks back at me wide-eyed. Then his gaze travels to his hand, and I follow it to the still-glowing sigil carving its way across it, my half-moon bright against his tan skin.

He starts to smile, something fierce lighting up his eyes. Then he waves his hand over the sword, turning it into an ice-blade ten times the original size, yet he carries it as if the weight is unchanged.

"Lend me your grimoire," he says. I summon the book to my hand and he presses his palm against it, spawning his own fiery-red butterfly wings, enhancing his strength and speed, and imbuing the sword with lightning magic.

"Hey you, you big glorified eel!" Kiran shouts at the monster and points his blade at him. "I'm going to seriously ruin your day."

He takes one step toward the monster, pauses, and looks back at me. "For the record, I need you too."

He kicks off from the ground and charges at the monster, avoiding its sharp bites and tail whips. He keeps slashing with the sword, but the ice shatters and has to be reformed with every swing. Finally, he baits the monster into trying to swallow him, and he stabs the ice blade into the gums of the beast, electrocuting it with the lightning magic imbued inside.

It feels strange to watch him—I can feel every bit of magic he uses as if I had cast the spells myself. He is like a knight of the moon. My moon. My knight.

The monster flails wildly to try and dislodge him as Kiran sheds the ice sword and starts carving loose one of his mighty fangs with the steel blade within.

The monster shakes Kiran loose and spits him out onto the beach, but as it rears up, an arrow zooms in from above, exploding into a ball of fire in the monster's eye.

The creature lets out a shrill roar of pain and turns away to dive back into the sea, but I summon the remnants of my strength to stop him. From the stars, pillars of light fall in a row, creating a plateau of ice too thick for the beast to dive through.

Kiran flies up to the monster's face before he can react and sinks his ice blade into another eye. The serpent bucks, throwing Kiran, but he recovers with a hard beat of his wings.

At that moment the oppressive force of the sea tugs at my senses, and I look back at the path down from the cliffs. Sure enough, Ms. Rivers is there, holding a sword in a black scabbard. The pommel contains an aqua-colored crystal held in place by tentacle designs wrapped around it.

She walks down the path, letting her hair down while her glasses turn to water and evaporate from her face. Her clothes change to black pants and a black bodice over her renaissance blouse. Finally, her cloak and hat form on her body from water.

"Thalassa Kaia Marina," Kiran says. "The Witch of the Seas, and Cyra's second in command!"

Ms. Rivers–Thalassa–unsheathes her sword. "Come, Leviathan!"

As the sea dragon's body turns to light and is absorbed by her ninjatō sword, the steel blade turns a shimmering blue, and she returns the sword to its scabbard.

Cara, Kiran, Celly, and I gather together on the beach.

"So, you made Kiran your vassal after all this time? You must trust him a great deal . . . or been terribly desperate," Thalassa mocks. "You are so like Yukiko, you know. Just as stubborn. But while Yukiko was quite possibly the greatest witch of her time, you are little more than a cheap imitation." She looks me up and down, nothing but disdain on her face. "What a disappointment."

"What does it say about you that us 'disappointments' have thwarted every one of your plans so far?" Kiran barks back.

"It says that I should have taken matters into my own hands from the start," she says. "But that is a mistake I will soon rectify. It is time for you to fall into the deep."

Her sigil glows for a moment, and a dreadful feeling forms in the pit of my stomach. As I turn, the wall of water speeding toward us is larger than anything I've ever seen. Its crest reaches the clouds, and its speed is incomparable. There is nowhere to go to avoid it, and in an instant, the entire sea comes crafting down on all of us, sweeping us out into the ocean's murky depths.

XXII.

Flood

As we are swept into the depths of the sea I look around, desperate for any solution to prevent us from drowning. My first thought would be to cast shadow bubbles over everyone's faces, but we'd still suffocate—the shadows don't create oxygen, they only create a barrier to block the water.

I have to think of something. There must be a solution.

I close my eyes and trust my senses. I search for the moon, but its presence does not exist at all here . . . which must mean that she's brought us into a subspace. But the magic of the half-moon exists inside me, so I must be able to draw it out somehow.

Sure enough, as I keep the half-moon in my mind, I can feel it materializing in this space, somewhere beyond the depths, joining us through its connection to me.

Please, I plead with the moon in my mind. *Please help us.*

As if answering my call, air starts to fill my lungs. It's a weird sensation, breathing through the water. It feels as though my spell is trading air from a shadow dimension, a space that exists alongside this one.

I use my senses to guide me to Celly first, who has no means of maneuvering underwater. I tuck them away and then follow my senses to Cara next, who looks befuddled by her sudden ability to breathe underwater.

I try to talk but my voice won't carry through the water, so I grab her arm and point toward Kiran's location.

The depths have terrible visibility. I can only see a few feet in front of me, so as I approach Kiran's location and a massive shadow comes into view, a part of me can't help but feel afraid of what it might be. I feel a shiver down my spine, mentally preparing to confront yet another deep sea monster.

As I get closer I realize it's a building . . . one I am well acquainted with by now. City hall.

Just above the clocktower is Kiran, and he looks back at us and starts swimming—but as we swim toward each other, powerful currents shift us around and drag us in different directions.

The current slams me into the wall of an apartment building, then hauls me around the town again. I struggle against it and desperately search for Kiran and the others with my senses, but it's too powerful. Finally, it pulls me to Thalassa, her cloak drifting suspended in the water and her face ghostly pale. She watches me with an eerie glow in her eyes, floating like a maritime ghost in the deep waters.

The current drops me in front of her. I try to move–to attack her, to swim away, to raise my hand–but a powerful pressure holds me in place. The pressure builds, squeezing my body until I can feel my bones bracing against the force, on the verge of snapping. I bite back a scream, fighting against the pain that's unlike anything I've ever felt.

There is nothing I can do in the water. As long as we are submerged, I am completely at her mercy. I need to change things—but how? My powers are drained from the battle on the shore. I have very little left.

This place is a subspace, and subspaces allow reality to be more easily manipulated—but what can I do to manipulate this space?

The answer waits for you where it has always been—in your dreams.

I think back to my dream. How the city looked, reflected in the sky waters. How it was so strange for the water and sky to be reversed–

That's it!

I concentrate all of my magical energy on my moon. And I imagine the city as if it exists on a flat plane. Then I imagine flipping that plane over.

I can sense the position of the moon changing, as if rotating around me. As it reaches below me the whole world starts to shake, and the waters become turbulent, slipping out of her control. The water pressure around me weakens and I start to move free. Thalassa looks around, confused, as I escape her attack and am swept away.

As the current brings me to an office building, I shatter the glass with a spear of ice and fight against the current to get inside, freezing my boots to the floor so I stay inside. As the water begins to drain out of the building, it causes all kinds of structural damage. Walls and entire floors below and above me collapse, almost every window shatters, anything that isn't nailed down is swept away, and I am left dangling as the city completely turns upside down.

Releasing my ice spell, I fall to the ceiling, which caves in and drops me to the ceiling below.

"Of course," I mutter under my breath. "Celly, are you there?"

They fly out of my pocket. "My regular cellular functions have sustained extensive water damage and can no longer be used, but I am otherwise unharmed."

With all the water gone, visibility has extensively improved. My senses tell me that Cara and Kiran both successfully avoided being swept away as well, though somehow I already knew that would be the outcome.

As I look around the ruins of the inverted city from the window, I spot Thalassa standing in the remains of city hall. Despite how exhausted and weak I feel, she's at a disadvantage right now. Perhaps I can catch her off guard.

I cast my wings and enhance my strength again. I used this move against Seath, and the only reason it failed then was that Seath is almost comically strong. Just like before, I use blasts of wind magic to kick off, propelling myself like a spear from the blast. But Thalassa casts a water barrier that absorbs my kick, and I back away.

"Oh, I'm sorry. Were you expecting me to be beaten so easily just because you drained the water?" she taunts. "I'm offended that you think so little of me, though I suppose Seath and Yukiko never told you who I am, did they?"

"How could they with your spell in effect?" I yell back. "You messed with all of our minds! And all for what? Just because of some disagreement Yukiko and Cyra had over a hundred years ago?"

"Yukiko was my coven sister! And she betrayed us! We were all sisters in the Coven of the Seven-Pointed Star, and Yukiko turned her back on all of us after our sisters Venus and Scarlett died."

"It doesn't matter anymore!" I shout. "Yukiko is gone!"

"Death was just one move on the game board, and it was not Yukiko's last one to play. As for you," she says with a malicious grin, "I have held my tongue for over thirty-five years. It's time I pay Seath back for what he stole from me!"

She raises her hand and fires a jet of water at me, but as I duck to avoid it she leaps forward with her sword and slashes my wings, her blade cutting right through the ethereal magic. It hurts like pulling teeth, but I try to ignore the pain. I run from her but she hits my back and I collapse.

As she approaches, a familiar sense catches my attention. Sure enough, the floor above bursts and Kiran drops down, slashing at Thalassa with his sword. She avoids the swing.

Kiran and I trade a glance as he pulls me to my feet.

I lay my sigil hand on Kiran's blade, imbuing it with flame and lightning, while I create my own ice blade, this time with it being tangible.

"Let's finish this," Kiran says.

XXIII.
Thalassaphobia

Thalassa's swordswomanship is better than even Seath's, and despite also dodging fire and lightning attacks from Celly and cutting down my shadow giants, she still keeps Kiran on his toes. It's all he can do to avoid being cut.

I try to create a barrage of ice spears from different directions, but her water barrier forms to intercept them.

Celly flies close to me. "I'm sorry, Selena, I don't have any strength left to fight," they say. Their avatar looks drained and their colors have grown dull.

"Find Cara then, she might need help," I command.

I, too, find myself drained and too weak to carry on, but I have no choice. As Thalassa corners Kiran at the edge of the roof, I summon the ethereal sword again, swinging it right through Thalassa's barrier and freezing it along with her body.

Kiran stumbles away from the edge to me, and we both step back as the ice around Thalassa begins to crack and break apart.

"I can't keep this up forever," Kiran says, breathing heavily and scowling. "Other than Cyra, Thalassa is the oldest witch in the Golden Coven. I can't hold her back much longer."

"I don't have any power left," I say, my voice starting to waver. "I don't know what to do."

"We could knock her over the edge," he says. "If you fall into the nothingness in a subspace, you die."

She created this subspace, she would surely dispel it before that happened, letting all of us out. It's a good plan.

We share a nod, and as Thalassa bursts from the ice, we both jump forward to try and push her to the edge, but she repels us easily. She's like a dancer, the way she glides and maneuvers her blade while manipulating jets of water around herself to intercept attacks and fire back. Every one of my offensive spells is dodged or blocked, and Kiran is completely outmatched in close range. Every second we spend dueling her just drains us further.

Thalassa fires a jet of water at me that knocks me toward the edge. I nearly roll off the side, but I manage to crawl away. As I look back, a ball of water collects on Kiran's wrists, locking his hands in place, and Thalassa easily strikes the sword from his hands.

She shoves him against one of the four support columns and presses her sword to his throat, and I scream, "Stop!"

As my heart pounds in my chest, I feel the shadows from the dark side of my moon emerging, growing wild inside.

She scoffs. "You think you can save his life just by whining like a spoiled little girl? How arrogant are you? Did Seath stop when I begged him not to take Alton from me? Did Yukiko stop when I pleaded with her not to leave us? How dare you think you could just cry and scream and I'd just spare him out of pity for you!"

"Please, you know what it's like to lose someone. Please don't hurt him," I plead, trying to suppress the furious darkness itching beneath my skin. "You weren't always like this, were you? The person I saw in Seath's memories, who cried for Alton—I don't think that person would do this. The person you were when you were my teacher wouldn't do this!"

"You naive, arrogant little brat," she spits. "You have no idea what I can do—what I *have* done. Do you really think your tears mean anything to me? You're not special."

As her arm begins to move, the raging shadows inside me burst out, and from my hand three shadowy chains fire out and bind Thalassa's arm. "I said *stop!*"

She looks back at me incredulously, and Kiran takes her moment of distraction to push the sword away. I see the ice forming on his left hand, taking the shape of a claw just like Seath's. He swings right for her, but in one fluid movement she coils my shadow chains around her sword and cuts them to shards, while her other hand catches Kiran's wrist.

She melts the ice claw to water, then increases the water pressure until Kiran lets out a scream and his wrist snaps in an unnatural direction. She steps behind him as he wails in pain and grabs him by the hair, pressing the blade to his back.

"Very well, you want to save him? I'll give you the chance," she says spitefully. "Jump. Jump over the edge, and I'll let him go."

If the situation were reversed, would Kiran even hesitate? I have to save him, no matter what. I can't let anything happen to my friends.

"I have your word?" I say, my voice quivering. I step closer to the edge, but my legs feel like lead weights.

"Don't!" Kiran yells. "She'd just kill me anyways, don't give her the satisfaction!"

"Shut up! You don't want to know all the ways I can make this worse for you, Kiran," she barks. "This is Selena's decision— jump, or I stab him through the heart and kill you next!"

I peer over the edge. Every fiber of my being screams at me to step away from the void. My legs shake and buckle, and even the sight of the clouds below rob me of my breath. I look back at her, but a peculiar sense suddenly calms me down.

Thalassa's eyes narrow for a moment, then she kicks Kiran away from her and spins on her heels. With superhuman speed she catches an arrow in mid-air, its red-hot tip mere inches from her face.

"Did you really thi–"

The arrow explodes in her face, causing her to recoil with a scream.

I can see Cara in a distant apartment building. She's not hurt! I wave my arms and shout for her. Out of the corner of my eye, I notice Kiran stumbling for his sword. He waves at Cara and points the blade at one of the support columns.

I'm not sure what he means until Cara fires another arrow. It turns into a sickening ooze just before impact that melts right through the concrete and rebar, eliminating one of the supports holding the clocktower up.

As Thalassa recovers, I turn to Kiran. "Use that giant ice sword! Trust me!"

He nods and casts it, but with the limited space, Thalassa easily blocks it with her own sword. I cast a fire spell in my hand and superheat Kiran's sword, just like how I defeated Thalassa's second thrall. The ice sword explodes and launches her back just as Cara eliminates another support.

The tower shakes and the ceiling starts to slope toward the void, throwing everyone off balance. I watch Thalassa stumble near the edge, but she plants her feet at the last second.

Cara takes out a third support, leaving only one remaining. The building groans and bits start to fall free. I don't think it can stay like this for long.

Kiran charges at Thalassa, swinging his sword one-handed, but she repels him with her blade.

As I sense Cara freeing her fourth arrow, I manipulate the wind to flip us both and freeze our boots to the floor above, just in time for Cara's arrow to destroy the last support beam.

The entire roof of the clock tower starts to descend into the void with Thalassa. This is it! The moment she lets us out of the subspace, we should attack with everything we've got.

But instead, she begins to levitate away from the debris, to our combined horror.

"Selena?" Kiran whispers calmly. I look at him and there is an uncomfortable aura of serenity in him. "Thank you for giving me this chance to be a vassal again. Look after Sovanna and the others."

"Wha–"

He smiles as he shatters the ice holding him in place, then kicks off with wind magic.

"Kiran!" I scream as he launches himself at Thalassa, sending them both crashing into the falling clock tower as he stabs his sword through her robe, pinning her to the ceiling.

I call for him as my tears drip away into the void, helplessly watching him and the tower fall below the clouds. As Kiran's presence disappears from my senses, it feels like all of my breath has been ripped from my body. I gasp and choke on my sobs, and stare at the emptiness below for a long time.

No matter how much I reach, how loudly I scream his name into the nothingness, he won't answer or come back. He's just gone.

Cara flies over with Celly, and I release my ice boots and reform my wings so I can join them on the next floor up in the city hall building. I drop to my knees at the edge of the destroyed wall, and stare out at the void. Cara drops down beside me, hugging me.

"Kiran fell," I choke out finally.

"I saw," she whispers.

From beyond the clouds, the powers of the sea remain. All at once Thalassa emerges, levitating higher and higher. Her sword is gone and her robe has a long tear in it, but she remains.

The sight of her causes the dark rage inside me to stir. I can feel an angry power coursing through me, despite my exhaustion. I wipe my red eyes and stare at her.

"What are we going to do?" Celly asks.

I stand up, my wings flaring wide behind me. "I'm going to hurt her."

XXIV.

Rage

I remain only partially conscious of my surroundings as our rampaging battle sends more and more chunks of the city into the oblivion below. I can feel the surge of power from the dark side of the moon running wild to fulfill my will, but I can't be bothered to even focus on what is happening.

How could Kiran just be gone like that? He sacrificed himself to defeat Thalassa, and it didn't even work. And nothing I do will bring him back to me. Even destroying her won't undo this.

I know I should be sad—*feel* sad, yet all I can feel is rage.

It's not fair. I didn't do anything to her, yet she came after *me*. She's hurt everyone I care about, and now my friend is *gone*. How could she do this to us? How could she hurt people who've done no wrong?

A thin layer of black fog rests around my whole body. It's translucent enough to see right through, but it manifests all of my attacks. A series of clouds form from the fog and grow dense and solid like stone. I launch these shadow meteors at Thalassa, but she either destroys them or dodges them—in either case, they explode in a wild, frenzied corrosive blast, sending more chunks of debris into the void.

It's all because of her.

I fire off countless chains in every direction to ensnare her while I dodge blasts of boiling water. My chains miss, so I recall them and empower my fist with dark energy. As she flies near the school, I launch myself at her.

It feels different from using the enhancement spell—this magic enhances my strength many times more but it also itches and burns, like insects crawling under my skin. The irritation only grows the rage inside me.

I release the build-up of anger and darkness as I punch through her water barrier, destroying it and blasting her back through the school walls. My attack provides momentary relief from the irritation in my skin, but with each passing second that maddening sensation comes back.

I spot Cara and Celly from the corner of my eye flying nearby as I soar into the school to investigate the hall she ended up in. She isn't there anymore, but I can sense her inside the building.

As I walk down the hall, her face appears in every window around me.

"You won't beat me," Thalassa mocks. "No matter how hard you try, I'm better at this than you."

I ignore her and try to pinpoint her location with my senses, but it's difficult. She seems to be suppressing her presence to hide from me.

"You must be close to completely burning out what's left of your power. This pitiful second wind is not nearly strong enough to overcome me."

I release a high-pitched scream that shatters all the glass in the school, breaking the illusion—only the broken glass stays suspended in the air.

Predicting her attack, I blast my way through the wall and fly out to avoid it as the shards fly toward me, chasing me. I create a corrosive shadow barrier to intercept the glass, reducing it to sand.

I feel Thalassa slam into me from behind, staying latched onto my back as she pushes me through the wall and crashing into our classroom.

She grips my wings and rips them off of my body, then starts dragging me by my hair. "You have learned a hard lesson today about persevering when it is hopeless and pointless to do so. Pity you're going to die before you can apply it. Give Kiran my best."

As she approaches the edge the floor collapses under her. I jerk away as her grip loosens and she falls through.

218

When I look I can see the ooze from Cara's acid arrows melting away more of the floor, and there Cara is, flying just outside the window.

As Thalassa tries to recover, Cara flies down a level and fires an ice arrow that bursts just above her, freezing her to the ground. As Thalassa frees herself from the ice, I jump down to her level and subdue her in shadow chains.

I slam Thalassa through walls. I smash her into desks and cupboards, into the floor and the ceiling, against every surface I can find, and each time her body crashes against something, the infuriating sensation in my skin is momentarily alleviated. I tighten the chains around her body as much as they will go without crushing her. Then I smash her through the outer wall and dangle her over the void.

One of my chains wraps around her throat and I make it restrict. Slowly that itch returns under my skin. I want to make it go away. I want to break her. I stare at her and she stares at me, defiant of my power over her.

Tighter and tighter the chain restricts, until her breathing turns to weak, ineffectual gasps and wheezing—then nothing. I can feel her getting weaker. I just scowl and clench the chains tighter.

"Selena," Cara says gently, landing next to me. "Selena, that's enough."

I hate Thalassa.

"You'll kill her," Celly says. "I recommend letting her go."

I don't want to let go.

"So what? She tried to do the same to us," I growl. "And Kiran . . ."

The mere mention of his name causes tears to blur my vision.

Cara places her hand on mine, and her touch instantly soothes the enraging sensation of my dark magic. "You don't have to be like her. You can always choose to be better. Be the person I know you can be."

I keep my eyes locked on Thalassa, and suddenly all I can see is her on that beach, cradling Alton. As I look back at Cara, I realize I am at the precipice of that exact moment. And all I'm doing right now is continuing the cycle. Everyone was hurt because of her. I shouldn't give in to my hatred the way she did. I shouldn't be like her. She's not the person I want to become.

I bring Thalassa back inside with my chains and release the one around her throat. She coughs and gasps for air, wheezing heavily.

As my anger starts to subside, my dark magic begins weakening and the exhaustion starts to come back.

"Let us out of this sub-space," I say. "This fight is over."

She glares at me. "Don't you dare look at me with that pitiful expression. I have waited thirty-five years to avenge Alton and make Seath suffer!"

"Alton is gone," I tell her. "And hurting me or Seath or anyone else won't bring him back. You being hurt doesn't mean you get to hurt other people. That's not how you heal, Thalassa."

"Just because you show me mercy doesn't mean I'll return the favor," she spits out.

"I know."

Thalassa sighs and closes her eyes, and the sub-space fades away to nothing.

We reappear back on the school rooftop, sometime before dawn. Seath is right where we left him, and a warm smile crosses his face when we reappear.

Behind Thalassa, the air seems to be cracking like broken glass. The glass-like effect shatters, revealing a woman in a black cloak and masquerade mask.

"Hello, sister," she hisses, placing her hand on my chains and turning them to dust.

"Velia!" Seath roars.

The cloaked woman simply grins from under her mask. "Sorry I can't stay and reminisce. I've merely come to take this young lady home."

"Big sis Cyra sent you?" Thalassa croaks. "But what about your mission?"

"You know you always come first."

A strange circle appears at the women's feet, with a sun symbol emitting a solar flare as its centerpiece surrounded with a triangle and three rings depicting different symbols in gold. With a snap of Velia's fingers, the women disappear in a burst of flame, and for a brief second, I can sense Cyra's aura . . . wherever they have gone, she is waiting for them.

I sigh and stumble back toward Seath. Cara and I both hug him tearfully, and I look up at him.

"Kiran fell, there was nothing . . . I . . ."

I pick up on a familiar sense and my head snaps toward the athletics field.

It couldn't be.

I pull away from Seath as if in a daze, stumbling to the edge of the roof. In the dark it's hard to see, but there's the field, and the bleachers, and two figures standing near them, and—

I gasp, tears blurring my vision, as I see Kiran standing beside my mom. They wave.

I don't even take the time to use the stairs. I leap right off the roof, counting on Kiran to brace my fall with magic. I land softly, impatiently pulling myself free of the spell and sprinting across the field as fast as I can. As he runs to me, too, I leap at him and throw my arms around him and he catches me and spins me in the air.

As Kiran sets me down we look at each other for a moment. Our eyes meet, and I instinctively draw him closer to me. I close my eyes, and just a moment after I feel his lips press against mine. It lasts for maybe a second at most, but it feels like an eternity. I feel like I'm melting into him.

I open my eyes, and I can feel my cheeks burning scarlet. "How?"

He shuffles away from me awkwardly, and gestures to my mom—whom I am only now realizing just saw every part of that—as she calmly walks toward me. "When I fell into the void, she pulled me free of the subspace with her magic."

"I could feel that he was in danger," Mom says. "I wanted to get all of you out, but I only had enough power to get Kiran. I'm sorry I couldn't do more to help."

I hug her next, squeezing her tightly. She did more than help. Everything is going to be okay because of her. "Thank you," I tell her.

As I look back, Cara and Celly emerge from the back door, and Kiran walks off to meet them.

"For the record," Mom whispers. "We are totally going to talk about that kiss later."

"Mom!"

She smiles mischievously. "Don't 'mom' me young lady, we are going to have some new ground rules while you're staying at Seath's house. No more closed doors, understand?"

As Seath finally joins us, limping his way over, I look around and take everything in. Everyone's okay, despite how hard the battle was. Cyra and Thalassa may still be out there, but for today, we've won.

XXV.
The Road Ahead

Cara and I rest on a rock by the lake, watching Kiran training with Celly off in the distance. The sun is bright and it's a cloudless day, but a cool breeze keeps us comfortable in the shade of a tree. Cara keeps lazily throwing a stick for Sovanna to fetch and bring back, and I thumb through some of the books from Yukiko's workshop.

"So, is Kiran still acting all awkward since you guys kissed?" Cara asks coyly.

"Ugh, yes!" I say, covering my face with my hands. "I don't know what's up with that, but he better figure it out soon because I'm way too embarrassed to make the first move. Is it crazy to expect him to ask me out?"

"Well, we don't say crazy, remember? No self-put-downs," Cara says. "And I don't think it's unusual, but it is an old-fashioned gender norm to have that expectation." She pauses for a moment, gazing into the distance. "It does feel weird now that his parents are back, you know, with him not sleeping in the house anymore," Cara says. "I miss his help in the kitchen."

It's been three weeks since Thalassa left. Not long after, Kiran's parents came back, and it's been peaceful ever since. It's nice. It feels like it's been so long since I've had the chance to just be ordinary and not have to worry about fighting.

But, of course, there are still a lot of unanswered questions. There's three other women in Cyra's Coven, there's Kiran's former friends, there's the question of Juniper—and then there's the whole matter of Yukiko's books.

I look through her notebooks. It's dense research, all dedicated to the study of resurrecting the dead. It's like she was obsessed with the concept. A lot of these notes are what seem to be her interpretations of research, and circles she discovered in her studies. She discovered spells to bind spirits to objects, spells to enable the spirit to control the dolls perfectly, spells to enable the spirit to communicate, spells to resist the effects of what she called *spirit corrosion,* and more. Much more.

From what I can tell, the mannequins, or dolls, as she called them, were more than just replicas. She intended for them to, once bound to a living soul, operate like a real living body. A lot of her own work seems to be based around this twin flame concept she theorized may succeed, but I don't really understand it, and her notes on the topic are incomplete.

"You know, according to this book, Yukiko found a way to transfer living souls into doll bodies. She thought it was the secret to bringing the dead back to life," I tell Cara. "I think she was planning on doing this to herself with the doll in the tower, but for whatever reason, she didn't end up doing it."

Cara hums. "Maybe Seath could make sense of those books. Have you asked him about it?"

"He gets cagey whenever I talk about Yukiko," I reply. "Still, this stuff was like an obsession of hers. I think it was some last-ditch effort to rid herself of the Sun's Curse."

"Kids!" Seath calls from the path to the house.

Cara and I both climb down, and I stretch my legs and back with a groan. Celly and Kiran catch up to us as we get closer to the house.

"Hey, Celly, Sovanna," Cara says suddenly. "Want to race to the house?"

"Cara!" I whine, but she looks back at me with a smug grin and takes off, the dog and Celly chasing her.

Kiran and I walk in a tense, heavy silence for a moment. He clears his throat twice, as if preparing to say something, but nothing comes out. From the corner of my eye I can see him stealing glances at me then looking away, as if he's embarrassed by the grin on his face. I take a deep breath and reach for his hand, burrowing mine in his.

"How are your parents?" I ask, trying to break the silence.

He sighs. "Mom is upset that Cyra wouldn't see her, but she says that probably means on some level, Cyra feels guilty over betraying me. It seems our family has been ex-communicated from the magical community over this. It's for the best, but it's still hurtful. All those people who work for Cyra or live within her community, they were our friends and neighbors."

"That must be awful. But it won't be forever. Maybe one day, we'll be able to get through to the others," I say.

We all gather inside the library, sitting around the table. As Seath groans and sighs in his chair, massaging his leg, I feel a pang of guilt.

"How is it?" I ask him.

He shrugs. "It's fine. Some days are worse than others, that's all. There's no sense whining about it."

"Why did you call us all here?" Kiran asks.

"Another lesson?" Cara suggests.

"No," Seath says. "We are outmatched when it comes to this conflict with the Golden Coven. And what's more, we're vulnerable to suffering a similar fate to Yukiko if we don't proceed with caution. We desperately need to teach you the art of cursewarding."

"Cursewarding?" I ask.

"It's a powerful but dangerous type of magic that is designed to absorb curses placed on you," Kiran explains. "Every witch in the Golden Coven has one active at all times to protect themselves."

"Before you ask, no, the wards cannot remove curses that are already in place, so it will not bring us any closer to overcoming the Sun's Curse," Seath adds.

Seath makes a laborious rise from his seat, and with his cane to help, he limps over to the windows.

"It's time I take you kids on a trip. When summer comes, we'll be heading out," he says.

"Where?" Celly asks.

"To see one of the few people still alive who can help us," Seath answers. "A witch who may just hate Cyra as much as I do. She was close to Yukiko, Cyra, Venus, and Thalassa back in the day—a sister from the Coven of the Seven-Pointed Star. And as far as I know, she is the only still-living member who is not allied with the Golden Coven."

He looks back at us and continues: "There are two problems, however. The first is that it has been a long time since I've seen her and she is not an easy person to find. The second problem is that she and I don't exactly get along. We had a falling out many years ago, and it's possible she still hates me. But she is an expert in cursewarding and someone who can help us defeat the Golden Coven."

"You still haven't told us where we'll be going," Cara points out.

Seath grins. "She lives deep within the Appalachians."

"Who is she?" I ask.

"Alice Alabaster, The Witch of Darkness."

The story will continue in . . .

Selena's Magica Somnia

Book 3: *The Witch in the Deep Woods*

A.V. Dawn

Scan the QR code below or visit lunarwillow.com to sign up for our monthly newsletter and get access to updates before anyone else, exclusive additional content, behind-the-scenes stuff, and deals. Staying connected helps us to keep creating new and exciting content! We appreciate your support.

www.ingramcontent.com/pod-product-compliance
Lightning Source LLC
Chambersburg PA
CBHW071148180726
48291CB00007B/2375